CHAOS IN LITTLE LEAF CREEK

A LITTLE LEAF CREEK COZY MYSTERY

CINDY BELL

CONTENTS

Chapter 1	1
Chapter 2	7
Chapter 3	14
Chapter 4	22
Chapter 5	31
Chapter 6	42
Chapter 7	49
Chapter 8	56
Chapter 9	63
Chapter 10	69
Chapter 11	77
Chapter 12	84
Chapter 13	91
Chapter 14	98
Chapter 15	105
Chapter 16	111
Chapter 17	117
Chapter 18	123
Chapter 19	131
Chapter 20	140
Chapter 21	149
Chapter 22	157
Chapter 23	165
Chapter 24	176
Chapter 25	183
Chapter 26	191
Chapter 27	199
Chapter 28	205

About the Author	215
Also by Cindy Bell	217
Tessa's Vanilla Cake Recipe	223

Copyright © 2020 Cindy Bell
All rights reserved.

Cover Design by Lou Harper, Cover Affairs

All rights reserved. No part of this publication may be reproduced or transmitted in any form or by any means, electronic or mechanical, including photocopy, recording, or any information storage or retrieval system, without permission in writing from the publisher.

This is a work of fiction. The characters, incidents and locations portrayed in this book and the names herein are fictitious. Any similarity to or identification with the locations, names, characters or history of any person, product or entity is entirely coincidental and unintentional.

All trademarks and brands referred to in this book are for illustrative purposes only, are the property of their respective owners and not affiliated with this publication in any way. Any trademarks are being used without permission, and the publication of the trademark is not authorized by, associated with or sponsored by the trademark owner.

ISBN: 9798665108087

CHAPTER 1

Cassie Alberta tucked a loose, brown curl back behind her ear and took a breath of the fresh air. Country air smelled different, and in some cases better. She had left behind the fumes of the city buses, but also the spice of the eclectic gathering of restaurants. In exchange she savored the scent of hay, mingled with the fertilizer it took to operate a farm. The farther into the small town she drove, the more the scents shifted. Fresh cut grass, the sweet scent of a local bakery, the heady aroma of sunbaked dirt on the side of the road. Summer was the worst time to move.

Cassie had discovered this quickly when hefting the items she hadn't wanted to put into the moving truck, into the trunk of her hatchback. Sweat trailed down the back of her neck, despite the cool air that blasted out of the vents in the dashboard.

Cassie's dark green eyes drank in the sight of the quaint shops that she passed at little more than a crawl. An ice cream shop, complete with hand-painted windows, and multi-colored wrought iron outside seating. A library positioned exactly in the center of town, with a mural that spanned the length of the front of the building. Children reading with thought bubbles above their heads, filled with fantastic scenes from their imaginations. It was the library that had drawn her attention in the first place.

Cassie had told the real estate agent a general idea of what she wanted from her new town. After many years living in a bustling city, she ached for the small town of her roots. But even the small town she had grown up in had transformed into something far different, with splashy buildings, and a highway that ran right through it. She described a picturesque place, quiet, with many small businesses, and a small population. She wanted a place she could call home, her real home. She'd spent so much time feeling like a transplant in her luxurious surroundings, and she hoped that moving to Little Leaf Creek would change that.

However, the looks from the people she passed sent a different message. The locals, mostly dressed in denim and t-shirts, sent odd looks in the direction of her hybrid car, and squinted through the windows at her unfamiliar face.

Cassie smiled at them.

They didn't smile in return. But for a young girl that giggled as her mother tugged her into a shop.

Cassie took another deep breath and reminded herself that it would take some time to blend in with the locals. She had plenty of time to spare. She turned down a side road, and passed a parade of small houses, each with a small fenced yard, and a lush, full garden. She wasn't sure if it was the library, or the row of homes, all different colors, and yet all so similar, that had made Little Leaf Creek the place she wanted to live. Perhaps it was every unique detail that the residents of Little Leaf Creek took the time to infuse into their homes.

As Cassie drove a little farther out, the houses and properties became larger. There, nestled between a portion of the creek, and a neighbor's home, stood her house. Her house. It belonged to no one else. Only her name was on the deed. That had taken some time to comprehend. Every decision she made about the two-story farmhouse would be hers, and hers alone. From the look of the faded paint, and the untended garden, she knew there would be a lot of decisions to make. But she was ready.

Cassie parked in the driveway and sat for a moment to gather her thoughts. Everything in her life had changed so quickly. She knew that was what she needed. She'd tried for a few months to let things go back to normal, but there was no normal anymore. She discovered that if she wanted normal, she'd have to invent a new one, and she'd set out to do just that. She walked around the outside of the house to look at her new house from every angle, then she climbed the stairs onto the front porch and felt the wood of the railing beneath her palm. Her stairs, her wood, her porch. The thoughts swirled through her mind as she turned to look across the wide and mostly barren front yard.

Cassie stood on the front porch and smoothed down the skirt of her sundress. The moving truck wouldn't arrive until the next day. She had enough in her trunk to get her by until then. However, she felt no urge to unpack. Instead, she wanted to savor the sensation of standing on her front porch. She ran her fingertips across the peeled paint on the railing and thought about what color she might like it to be.

Michael had always liked red. Red ties, red cars,

even red curtains. She was happy enough to allow him his preferences, as she didn't have too many of her own. Now, she had to figure out what it was that she liked.

Cornflower blue, like the shade of her dress? She looked from the material, to the railing, then shook her head. She wouldn't want to take any blue away from the sky.

Cassie stepped out from under the awning that stretched across the porch and looked up at the bright sky. If it weren't for the quaint town, and the artistic touches throughout the town, the sky would have sold her on the location. Somehow it seemed bigger here. Maybe because there were no skyscrapers to interrupt it. She noticed a small plane in the distance. It flew over what appeared to be unending farmland. She wondered about the pilot inside. Could he see her? She waved, just in case, then laughed at herself for the silliness of it all.

"Time to get to work, Cassie." She walked across the front yard and back to her car. As she opened the trunk, she heard a sharp bark. She looked to the side and noticed a dog poking his nose through the slats of the wooden fence that surrounded her neighbor's yard.

"Hi there, pooch." Cassie smiled at the dog. "Don't worry, I'll stay right over here."

Cassie never had a pet in the city, their lifestyle didn't coincide with taking care of other living creatures. But when she was a little girl, living in a town where the roads were made of dirt and the buildings had all begun to sink, she'd collected neglected and wounded animals. Much to the disdain of her mother, she'd harbor them all in her bedroom and nurse them back to health. Whether it was an injured squirrel, or a skinny cat, she always found a way to help them.

"Maybe I'll get a pet." The thought brought a smile to her lips.

CHAPTER 2

As Cassie hauled a few boxes up to the front porch, the dog continued to watch her. He barked now and then but seemed content to mostly watch her come and go.

As Cassie lugged the last box onto the porch, she noticed the dog had been quiet for some time. She glanced over at the fence and saw no sign of him.

"I guess I'm not that interesting after all." She laughed, then began carrying her boxes into the house. On her way back out to get the last one, she found the dog, seated right next to it, on her porch.

"Uh oh!" Cassie stared at the dog. He had brown and white fur and pointy ears. He looked like a collie mix. "Are you an escape artist, is that it?" She looked over at the fence and noticed a pile of loose dirt that had been dug away from the bottom of the fence. "You sneaky thing." She held her hand out to the dog.

The dog gave it a sniff, then a lick.

"You know, it's not going to make a good first impression if my new neighbors think I stole their dog." Cassie gave him a quick pet. "Come on you, it's time to get back home." She hooked her fingers around his collar and guided the dog back toward the fence. She walked the length of it until she came to a small gate at the back of it. She grasped the rusty latch and gave it a light tug. It moved easily, allowing the gate to swing open.

Relieved, Cassie nudged the dog through the gate, then started to close it. Before she could, two goats burst through it, and out into the open field that backed up to the fence.

"Oh no!" Cassie gasped as the goats pranced with joy. The dog ran out as well, and began to bark at and chase the goats.

This certainly wasn't what Cassie had expected on her first day in her new home. As she watched the dog chase the goats, and the goats dodge the dog every time, she wondered for just a second if all of it might be a strange dream. But the sharp bark of the dog brought her focus back to reality. She had to do something, and fast.

It would make a terrible first impression with her neighbors if she lost the dog and goats before she'd even had a chance to introduce herself.

"Get back here!" Cassie rushed toward the goats in an attempt to scare them back through the open gate. Instead they kicked up their legs and ran in the opposite direction. The dog barked loudly and chased them from the other side, which sent the goats running straight toward her. She just managed to jump out of the way before they would have collided with her. The sudden movement of her jumping out of the way startled the goats, and they bolted off in the other direction again.

"Stop, please!" Cassie groaned as the dog chased the goats farther into the field behind the house. If there was ever a time when she wished she could melt into the ground, it was then. If only she had the chance to start her day all over again, maybe she could avoid this horrible situation. But the fact was, she had to hunt down the goats before they could get too far away.

Cassie ran in a wide circle around the goats and the dog. She couldn't get the goats to go through the gate, but her presence prevented them from running any farther through the field.

"It's time to go back home, goats!" She pleaded

with the animals and shooed them in the direction of the gate. Her heart skipped a beat as it looked as if they might actually cooperate. But an instant later, they ran off in two different directions.

"What's going on out there?" A gruff voice shouted from the back porch of the house.

"I'm so sorry!" Cassie looked up at the woman who walked down the steps and through the yard, toward the open gate. She walked with an uneven gait, favoring her right leg. Her silver hair framed her face in layered waves. She had weathered skin and looked to be in her sixties. "Your dog and goats are loose and I'm trying to get them back inside, but I'm not that familiar with goats, and they don't seem to like me much!" She lunged for the goats again, but the heel of her shoe snagged in the soft soil and snapped off, causing her to fall forward right onto the ground. She pushed herself up as the dog and goats all hurried over to sniff at her curiously. She winced as the dog licked her cheek.

"Alright now, that's a good boy, Harry." The woman reached down and shooed the dog away from Cassie. Then she offered her hand to Cassie. Her striking blue eyes settling on her. "Sorry, he's a friendly boy."

"Thank you." Cassie grabbed her hand and

managed to get to her feet. "I'm the one that should apologize. I should have just told you that Harry got out."

"Oh yeah, he opened up the gate, did he?" She eyed her from beneath furrowed eyebrows.

"No, I opened the gate actually." Cassie took a sharp breath as she tried to form a clear explanation.

"So, you are the one that let my goats and my dog out?" She looked past her, at the house beside hers, then shook her head. "I heard I was getting a new neighbor. Would that be you?"

"It's me, Cassie. Cassie Alberta." She winced. "But I really didn't mean to let the goats out, and no, I didn't let Harry out. You see, I think he was excited when he saw me arrive, and he dug his way out from under the fence."

"Not again." She grunted. "I've been trying to keep this dog fenced in for over a year. He always finds a way out. I'll be sure to fix that hole." She looked down at the dog seated in front of her. "You've got to stop being so friendly. That's not the way we do things around here."

"He's so sweet." Cassie laughed.

"I'm serious." She turned her attention back to Cassie. "Now look here, Cassie Alberta. I know that you're not from around here, and I'm sure that you have no idea who I am, but you'll hear plenty about me soon enough, and I want you to keep one thing in mind whenever someone tells you something about Tessa."

"Oh, don't worry, I would never believe gossip." Cassie waved her hand as she took a slight step back from her.

"You keep in mind that everything everyone says about me is true." Tessa looked straight into her eyes. "I like my privacy. I like to be left alone. If you're going to be my neighbor you're going to need to get used to that real fast." She slapped the outside of her thigh hard enough to make a loud cracking sound.

Cassie jumped at the sound.

The goats and dog bolted inside the fence. Tessa snapped the gate shut, then she turned and stalked back up onto the porch, and through the door.

Cassie dusted off as much of the dirt as she could from the skirt of her sundress, and sighed as she looked up at the tightly closed door. As far as first impressions went, she thought that might have been one of the worst. Dizzy from the entire encounter, and covered in a thin sheen of sweat, she stepped inside the house to wash up. Although she had a few changes of clothes, most of her wardrobe was on the moving truck. She found a pair of denim shorts and a tank top and grabbed her brush as she headed into the bathroom. When she turned on the water in the bathtub, the faint shriek that emitted from the faucet surprised her, but the loud shaking that followed made her jump back. When water finally dripped from the end of the faucet, the thickness and color of it shocked her.

"No, no, no!" Cassie groaned. She'd taken all of the steps to have the house inspected. She'd been assured there were no serious repairs to be done. Clearly, there was one very important issue.

Cassie turned the faucet back off and quickly changed. With a bit of dirt still smudged on her elbows she left the house behind. She hoped a drive into town would help take her mind off the embarrassing encounter with her neighbor. Now, she was on a mission. She had to find a plumber.

CHAPTER 3

*A*s Cassie eased her car through town, she noticed more people on the sidewalks than when she had driven in. Many appeared to be out for an early lunch, or simply enjoying a nice stroll. She couldn't help but relax a bit as their laid-back nature emanated from them.

Cassie pulled into the parking lot of Paul's Hardware, and parked near the entrance. She hoped that Paul would have some good advice on who to call about the plumbing problem. As she reached for the door handle, another hand pressed against the handle on the inside, and the door nearly swung into her.

"Sure thing, Paul! Right away!" The person on the other side of the door gasped as the door narrowly missed striking Cassie. "I'm so sorry, ma'am." The man pulled off his baseball cap and revealed a cascade of straight, blond hair that hung loose over his dark brown eyes. "I didn't see you there."

"It's alright." Cassie offered a short laugh. "I seem to be having some trouble staying upright around here."

"Is that so?" He squinted at her, his lips curled into a half-smile. "That accent. You're not from Little Leaf Creek, are you?"

"Is it that bad?" Cassie scrunched up her nose and wondered how she must sound to him. His own voice had a country drawl that made her think of home-baked bread and humid summer nights. Did hers conjure up images of taxis with blaring horns and crowded sidewalks?

"Not bad at all." He lowered his eyes for a moment, then looked back up at her. "Where are my manners?" He held his hand out to her. "Sebastian Vail, it's a pleasure to meet you."

"You as well, Sebastian." Cassie smiled as she took his hand. His rough skin grazed against the smoothness of her palm. The touch made her feel a bit giddy. She gazed into his eyes for a long moment.

"Well then." Sebastian's smile spread wider as he

drew his hand away. "I guess I'll just have to keep calling you ma'am."

"Huh?" Cassie laughed, an awkward sound that ended in an even more awkward cough. "Oh right, sorry. I'm Cassie."

"Cassidy?" Sebastian asked.

"No, just Cassie. Well, Cassandra. But everyone calls me Cassie." She continued to wonder what had caused her to become a bit giddy around him. "I'm sorry, Sebastian, it's been a rough morning. I've run into some plumbing problems, and it's only my first day here."

"Oh, you bought the place next to Tessa's?" Sebastian's eyebrows shot up, then he winced.

"You make it sound like a wonderful decision." Cassie managed a smoother laugh.

"I know the place could use some work, and so could your neighbor." Sebastian tipped his head back toward the store. "You weren't planning on doing it yourself were you?"

"And if I was?" Cassie's heart pounded a little harder. She'd spent so many years of her life with people assuming what she was capable and not capable of, defensiveness arose quickly in reaction to the grimace on his face.

"No offense intended." Sebastian pulled his cap

back down on his head. "It's just quite a job, that one there. If you could use some help, I'd be willing."

Cassie narrowed her eyes as she looked over the dirt smudges on his shirt, the mud caked to his work boots, and the holes in his worn jeans.

"You don't look much like a plumber." She paused. "No offense intended."

"I'm pretty sure I'd be offended if you thought I did." Sebastian chuckled then stepped all the way out through the door. "I'm not a plumber by trade. I'm a farmer. But I know my way around just about every part of a house, pipes included." He held up his hands. "But I understand if you'd rather hire a professional. There aren't too many around here, but I'm sure you could get someone out to look at it in a few days."

"A few days?" Cassie groaned, then closed her eyes. "Oh, this day is just getting better and better."

"It should be." Sebastian shifted from one foot to the other, then slid a little closer to her as he lowered his voice. "Your knight in shining armor just offered you free labor."

Although the words struck her as a bit odd, if not cheesy, the accent that wrapped around each one lulled her mind into a place it hadn't been since before she was married. Was he flirting with her?

Did he not know that she was rounding the corner to forty? A quick assessment of his mostly smooth skin and youthful smile made her think he wasn't quite in his thirties.

"I would have to pay." Cassie looked straight into his eyes.

"If you insist, I would never argue with a lady." Sebastian gave her a quick wink. "I'll be over in a couple of hours, just a few stops to make. Sound alright to you?"

"It sounds great. Here is my number in case anything changes." Cassie wrote down her number on a piece of paper and handed it to him, then breathed a sigh of relief and shook her head. "And thank you. It's very kind of you to offer."

"Neighbors help neighbors around here. That field that backs up to your house, that belongs to me." Sebastian stepped past her and started down the sidewalk. "Good to meet you, neighbor."

"You too." Cassie turned and watched him walk over to an old, beat-up pickup truck, the back of which was littered with tools and supplies. Briefly she wondered if she should let him help her try to fix the plumbing. Had she let his accent distract her from common sense? What if he made things worse?

Cassie took a deep breath and forced down her

panic. She was determined not to let her day get any worse. A few bumps in the road didn't have to ruin everything. She needed a good distraction, something to remind her of why she'd taken this giant leap, before it began to feel like a giant mistake.

As Cassie walked along the sidewalk in front of the hardware store, she peered into the windows of the store beside it. A variety of handmade items were on display, from jewelry, to handbags, to cute animal-shaped hats. The sight of them brought a smile back to her lips. Yes, this is what she wanted. Not mass-manufactured things, but the unique, one-of-a-kind creations of people with passion for their work. She was tempted to go inside to have a closer look, but a sharp sound drew her attention. She rounded the corner of the shop and found a wide alley, well-lit by the sun that shone above. A man stood toward the end of the alley, a blow torch in his hand, which he had aimed at a pile of misshapen metal in front of him.

Cassie paused as she watched him maneuver around the metal.

The metal began to take shape beneath the movements of the artist. She stepped to the side to avoid the spray of embers.

"Ugh, that terrible noise." A male voice called out from behind her.

Cassie glanced over her shoulder and spotted a couple who looked to be in their sixties hovering near the end of the alley. She put on her brightest smile. Maybe she could make at least one good impression.

"Hello there." The man returned her smile. "You're a new face, aren't you?"

"Oh, you must be Cassie. I'm Rose." The woman walked over to her and took her hand. "I've heard so much about you."

"You have?" Cassie raised her eyebrows as she wondered just what kind of rumors were already flying around.

"Oh, just that you're new to town, and you're stuck living next to Tessa Watters." Rose winced. "Sorry about that."

"I'm sure we'll do just fine." Cassie took a deep breath. "I'm glad to be here." She glanced over at the artist as he continued to work. "I love all of the creativity that flows through this place."

"It is a creative place." Rose scrunched up her nose as she shook her head. "But this kind of art I just don't understand."

"No?" Cassie took a few steps back to stand

beside her as she looked at the work in progress. "All I see is passion and creativity."

"I guess maybe I'm just too old for these things." Rose waved her hand. "I do try to keep up, but it seems I'm never on top of the trends these days. Maybe you could help me out with that." She gave Cassie's shoulder a light pat.

"I'm not sure I can keep up, either." Cassie laughed as she relaxed under the woman's warm touch. Maybe she'd end up with a friend or two after all. "But I'd be happy to try to help."

"Rose, we have to get going." The man beside Rose took her hand.

"Oh Charles, let's just watch a little longer. I'm sure that something wonderful is going to come out of all of this noise." Rose looked over at Cassie. "Right?"

"Right." Cassie grinned.

"If you insist." Charles sighed but smiled at Rose.

CHAPTER 4

A few minutes later the artist stepped away from his creation. He lifted the shield from his face and gazed at the metal in front of him.

Cassie noticed that he looked young, maybe barely over twenty. She felt a pang of envy that he had such talent at a young age, and such passion for his work. Finding her own talent was one of her goals for her new life.

"That's it?" Rose whispered.

"It looks like he's done." Charles shrugged.

"But it's just a twisted bunch of metal." Rose shook her head as she looked it over. "Just think of how much time and energy was wasted on this."

"I think it's quite pretty actually." Cassie smiled as the sunlight danced across the various angles and plateaus of the metal surface. "Look at the way it catches the light. Have you ever seen anything like it?"

"Only after a five car pileup." Charles waved his hand as he laughed. "It's not art, it's just mangled metal."

Cassie caught sight of the young man's expression as he looked over at them. She guessed that he had heard what Charles said, as his face grew tense.

"I think it's beautiful." Cassie smiled at the artist as he strolled over to them. "Is it for sale?"

"Yes." He cleared his throat nervously. "Are you interested?"

"Let's go, Charles. I want to get a seat at Mirabel's before it gets too crowded." Rose hooked her arm around Charles' arm and steered him away from the assortment of art.

"Yes, I am interested." Cassie gazed at the twisted metal again. "Does it have a name?"

"Rainbow." He shrugged. "Or you can call it whatever you want."

"Rainbow is perfect." Cassie glanced up at the sun, then looked back down at the metal sculpture. "I know exactly where I want to put it, too."

"But I haven't told you the price." He frowned as

he slipped his hands into his pockets. "Maybe, forty?"

"Forty?" Cassie narrowed her eyes as she walked around the creation. "It probably cost you more in supplies."

"Most of it is recycled metal. I harvest it from the dump outside of town." He lowered his voice. "I'd take thirty, if forty is too much."

"What's your name?" Cassie paused in front of him and looked into his eyes.

"Trevor. Trevor Danel." He brushed a few strands of his sandy brown hair away from his dark eyes, revealing the scabs and scars on his hand. She guessed they were from creating his artwork.

"Trevor, you shouldn't sell yourself short." Cassie held his gaze as she spoke in a firm tone. "Be proud of your work, and ask for what it's really worth, not for what you think someone might be willing to pay."

"Oh well, I don't know." Trevor shoved his hands back into his pockets. "It's not like I'm famous or anything. I just pump gas."

"Maybe you pump gas, but you're also an artist." Cassie reached into her purse and pulled out her wallet. She looked over what she had inside, then confidently pulled out two twenties. "Consider this a deposit. If you can deliver the art to my home, and help me install it, then I will give you another forty. And by the way, that's a deal for what you've done here."

"Are you sure?" Trevor stammered as he accepted the money. "That's a lot of money."

"And your art is worth a lot more than that." Cassie jotted down her address and phone number on a slip of paper and handed it over to him. "I can't wait to see how it looks in my front yard."

"Oh, you might not want to do that." Trevor took the paper as he shook his head. "The historical society around here is pretty strict about what can be put on your property."

"Oh? Well, let me handle them." Cassie smiled. "See you soon, I hope."

"Absolutely, I'll have it over there by about five tonight." A broad smile spread across his lips. "Thank you so much."

"Thank you, for creating it. Keep it up." Cassie waved to him, then continued down the street. Her heart warmed with the idea that she had inspired a young artist, but she was also very excited to see the artwork gather and reflect the sunlight in her front yard. She guessed it would splay an array of interesting shapes and colors against the front of her house. She was proud of making a choice that was just for her. When she walked past the diner, she suddenly felt hungry and decided to go inside.

As Cassie stepped into the diner, she noticed Rose and Charles at a table with a few other people.

"Over here, Cassie!" Rose waved to her. "It's just about the last seat in the house."

Cassie noticed that Rose was right. Most of the tables and booths in the diner were occupied with what she guessed were locals eager to enjoy their lunch. She'd read about Little Leaf Creek being mostly a bedroom town, with those that didn't work in the area, commuting an hour or two to do so. Clearly it had quite a retirement community as well, as many of the people in the diner were of retirement age.

"Thanks so much." Cassie walked over to the table.

"This is Miles, Karen, and Avery." Rose gestured to the three other people seated at the table.

"It's nice to meet you." Karen smiled at her. Her kind face was framed by tight, white curls. Beside her, Avery kept her nose buried in her menu. She appeared to be in her forties with wavy, blonde hair that settled on her shoulders.

"You too." Cassie settled into the chair and set her

purse in her lap. "Little Leaf Creek is such a wonderful town."

"You can tell she's not from around here." Miles chuckled. His loud laughter was in sharp contrast to his short stature. His black hair was piled on the top of his head with a good helping of silver streaks mingled through. "Let me guess, it's quaint?"

"It is." Cassie's smile faded some as the others all focused their attention on her. She knew she had to get used to being the latest spectacle in town, she guessed they didn't get too many newcomers. "I spent almost twenty years living in the city, and moving here, feels like coming home."

"I'm so glad you feel that way." Charles set down his glass of water and stared at her. "So many people want to change so much. They don't understand the value of small towns anymore. Even our young folk, as they grow up, they're always rallying to change things, build more, bring in bigger businesses. They just don't know how rare a place like Little Leaf Creek is."

"Exactly." Cassie sighed as she leaned back in her chair. "All of the local businesses, the pride that everyone takes in their homes, the air of community all around. It's just what I need after spending so many years in a fast-paced city."

"It's a big change though, isn't it?" Avery lowered her menu and looked across the table at Cassie. "Something drastic must have happened to bring you here."

"Avery, you shouldn't pry." Karen huffed as she looked over at her friend. "It gives the wrong impression."

"Well, either she can tell me the truth, or I'll just believe the rumors that we all know will be spreading in no time around this town." Avery shrugged as she looked back at Cassie. "I just wanted to give her the chance to speak up first."

Cassie's throat grew thick with words that she wasn't ready to speak. She glanced away from Avery, relieved to see a waitress walking toward their table. Immediately, she could see the warmth in the woman's blue eyes as they met hers.

"Would you just look at you!" She gasped and gave Cassie's cheek a light pat. "I heard the rumors about you, but none of them said how darn pretty you are."

"What?" Cassie laughed as she drew away from the woman's touch. But it didn't make her uncomfortable. In fact, the warmth of her fingertips lingered on her cheek even after her hand was gone.

Cassie took comfort from it, as if she'd already been welcomed into her family.

"This is Mirabel." Rose rolled her eyes as she smiled. "She's a bit much to take at first, but she grows on you."

"Oh, thanks so much, Rose." Mirabel grinned as she pulled an order pad out of the pocket in her apron. "Sorry it took me so long to get over here, but we're very low on staff. People keep moving away." She rolled her eyes. "Like it's really so much better anywhere else."

"It's no trouble." Cassie ordered a coffee. She noticed that Mirabel's long, red braid had a few glimmers of gold in it. "Apparently your diner is a popular place."

"Oh, it's not mine." Mirabel waved her hand and laughed.

"But your name is Mirabel?" Cassie's eyes widened. "Isn't that the name of the diner?"

"It used to be called Little Leaf Creek Diner. But the owner of it thought re-naming it after me would make me sweet on him." Mirabel tapped her pen lightly against her order pad. "Foolish man."

"Foolish enough that you married him." Miles spoke up with a smug smile.

"So, it worked?" Cassie grinned. She enjoyed the

jovial energy that bounced back and forth throughout the group.

"Foolish enough that I divorced him, too!" Mirabel put her hands on her hips as she glared playfully at Miles.

"And you still work here?" Cassie stumbled over her words as she attempted to keep up with the revelations.

"Sure, I love this place, just not him. He lets me run it while he runs around the world with his new wife." Mirabel winked at Cassie. "It might not be too traditional, but it works for us."

"Well, then it's what's best." Cassie grinned at her. She couldn't resist. Mirabel's enthusiasm felt contagious.

"I'll bring you the special, trust me, you'll love it." Mirabel looked at the others and began to take each of their orders. Once she had them all, she headed back toward the front counter and the kitchen behind it.

Cassie watched her go. Despite the pressure of being the only server working, she bounced as she walked and spared a smile to everyone she passed. Cassie admired that kind of determination to be positive. It bolstered her own mood quite a bit, as she looked back at the others around her.

CHAPTER 5

"So, tell me about this historical society I've been hearing about." Cassie met Rose's eyes. "Are they really so bad?"

"Bad?" Miles sputtered. "What makes you think they're bad?"

"Well, I just purchased a piece of art to place on my property, but the artist I purchased it from seemed to think that I would need permission from this historical society in order to install it there." Cassie glanced around at the others. "Have you heard of it?"

"Have we heard of it?" Avery laughed.

"I don't know, have we, Rose?" Charles grinned at his wife.

"I guess you have?" Cassie looked between the amused faces as she tried to catch up with the joke.

"Yes, we have, dear." Rose patted her hand. "In fact, you're sitting with quite a few members of it."

"I am?" Cassie's eyes widened as her heart began to race. "I'm sorry, I didn't mean to offend any of you."

"Relax. It's fine." Miles sat back in his chair as his food was delivered.

Cassie had a few seconds to stew on her mistake as Mirabel handed out their meals. Despite her embarrassment, she couldn't help but admire the swift and efficient movement of their waitress.

"If you need anything else just give me a yell." Mirabel lowered her voice as she looked at each of them. "And I mean that, because if you don't yell, I might not hear you."

"We'll yell." Miles locked eyes with her, then looked over at Cassie. "So, about this piece of art."

"It's quite beautiful." Cassie frowned as she felt the attention focus back on her.

Charles cleared his throat.

"Where do you plan to put it, dear?" Rose sweetened her voice.

"In the front yard." Cassie shifted in her chair. "There's such a big open space, and I'm sure the sun will hit the surface of the statue just right to create a stunning effect."

"In the front yard?" Miles scooted forward in his chair as he stared at her.

"I think it will be perfect." Cassie smiled at the thought.

"Oh no, that's not going to work at all." Avery shook her head. "You'll need approval for that."

"What do you mean?" Cassie narrowed her eyes.

"Anything facing the street must meet certain standards." Charles tapped his fingertip against the table. "We must present a uniform image, a representation of the historical value of this town. If we allow people to put whatever they want in their front yard, our town will lose its historical feel."

"That seems a bit extreme. I don't remember hearing about these rules when I bought the house." Cassie did her best to keep her voice even and polite. She didn't want to make any enemies on her first day.

"Don't worry, sweetheart, I'll help you figure all of this out." Rose gave the back of her hand a light pat.

"Great, thank you." Cassie's heart dropped as she wondered if that meant she would get to have her way, or if Rose would manage to convince her against it. "I'm sure if you could see it, where I plan to put it, you would see that it wouldn't be an eyesore of any kind or draw attention away from the history of the town."

"Actually, that sounds like a fantastic idea. I'll come by this evening and have a look at it. Then we can decide from there. But do understand, if the historical society votes against the statue, you will have to take it down." Miles looked around at the other people at the table as each one nodded.

Cassie frowned as she glanced around at the others.

"And who exactly is in charge of the historical society?"

"No one is in charge exactly." Avery shrugged.

"But we're all part of it. Along with a few others." Charles met her eyes as he smiled. "Don't worry, we're a fair bunch. We'll make sure that your artwork gets a fair trial."

Cassie winced at the thought. She recalled the way Rose and Charles had responded to the artwork when they first saw it. It was clear that they were not going to be on her side. However, she hoped that their quick friendship might steer them in another direction.

Cassie looked down at the food on her plate

which consisted of pasta and chicken and what appeared to be an alfredo sauce. The scent of it was enough to make her mouth water. At least she could enjoy that. However, as she went to pick up her fork, she realized that she didn't have any silverware on the table. Everyone else had already begun eating. She guessed that due to her joining them at the last minute there hadn't been a setting for her at the table.

Cassie looked up and spotted Mirabel near the register.

"Mirabel!" She called out.

Mirabel continued to focus on a few customers that were at the counter. A quick glance around allowed Cassie to spot a tray of rolled silverware on the end of the counter near the entrance of the kitchen. Instead of bothering the busy waitress, she decided to help herself. As she stood up and walked over to the tray, Mirabel spotted her and hurried over.

"Oh no, did I forget to get you silverware?" Mirabel groaned as she snatched up a roll before Cassie could grab it. "Please forgive me."

"There's nothing to forgive." Cassie met her eyes. "I think you're doing an amazing job."

"Well, aren't you just the sweetest." Mirabel tilted

her head to the side. "If you're not careful, I might just decide to keep you."

Cassie laughed at the comment as she accepted the silverware from Mirabel.

"You might want to hold off on that decision, I'm not making the best impression around here today."

"You've made a wonderful one on me. So sorry, it's not usually like this." Mirabel wiped her forearm across her forehead and sighed. "I've been trying to hire someone, but most of the college kids are going away for school, there are just slim pickings at the moment."

"Maybe I could give you a hand?" Cassie glanced back at the table, eager to escape being the topic of conversation. "I'll need a job soon enough, and I've been a waitress before." She swallowed hard as she held back just how long it had been since the last time she put on an apron.

"Seriously?" Mirabel gazed into her eyes, her mouth half-open. "Do you really want to work here?"

"Sure, it seems like a great place. It'll give me a chance to get to know everyone." Cassie shrugged. "I mean, if you'll have me of course."

"Do you want to start right now? I can get you an

apron." Mirabel laughed as she headed back around the counter.

"Uh, sure I can do that." Cassie trailed after her as her heart raced. She hoped that Mirabel wouldn't notice just how rusty she was. She'd spent two years working as a waitress in her hometown before she'd gone off to college. That was over twenty years ago. She guessed a few things had changed. "I might need a little refresher on things." She cleared her throat.

"Oh hon, don't worry. All you have to do is take the orders and try not to spill hot soup in anyone's lap. Other than that, it's mostly putting on a friendly show for the customers. They like to be wooed." Mirabel handed over a bright green apron with Mirabel's printed across the front. "You can work for cash today and we'll get all of the paperwork straightened out tomorrow."

"Okay." Cassie draped the apron over her head and tied it behind her back. She looked longingly at the food on her plate. She guessed it would taste just as good reheated. The important thing was to make sure Mirabel wanted to keep her. She needed one friend in this new town, and she had a strong suspicion that Mirabel would be it.

As Cassie began to help the diners, she met the cook, Frankie, who had a strong sense of humor and plenty of patience for her lack of knowledge. However, a lot of her time working as a waitress resurfaced as she took orders and delivered food. She remembered to smile, to always say yes, and to make sure the food was hot before she set it on the table. By the time the lunch rush came to an end, she was winded, and her feet had already begun to hurt. She would have to dig out a good pair of comfortable shoes when the moving truck arrived the next day. Thinking of the moving truck reminded her of the plumbing issue at her house, which reminded her of Sebastian.

"Oh no!" Cassie gasped as she looked at the clock on the wall.

"What's wrong? Hot soup in someone's lap?" Mirabel tossed a towel over her shoulder as she walked up to Cassie. "I can't thank you enough for all of your help. Now that the crowd is down, we can take a breath."

"I hate to do this to you, Mirabel, but I'm supposed to be meeting someone at my house to fix a plumbing problem." Cassie began to pull off her apron. "Actually, I was supposed to meet him some time ago. He's probably not even there anymore." She looked around the diner. "My purse?"

"Oh, it's right here." Mirabel grabbed it from

behind the counter and gave it to Cassie. "You left it at your table when you came to help me. Avery handed it in to me before she left because you were busy."

"Thank you." Cassie pulled out her phone, then sighed. She winced at the texts that scrolled across her screen. "I think he might still be there."

"You'd better get over there. Don't worry about it. It'll be quiet until dinner, and I have another waitress coming in then. You got me through the rush, and I am so grateful for it. We can work out your schedule once you're more settled in." Mirabel peered over her shoulder at the texts. "Oh, I know that number, is it Sebastian you stood up?"

"You know him?" Cassie looked up from the rushed apology she had been typing out.

"Oh honey, everyone knows Sebastian." Mirabel winked. "Or at least, we'd all like to get to know him better." She shook her head as she laughed. "It's going to be a new experience for him to be stood up with the way the ladies fall all over him around here."

"He is cute, isn't he?" Cassie laughed. "And apparently he has the patience of a saint, because he's still waiting for this old lady."

"Old lady?" Mirabel gave her a playful shove. "I've

never seen an old lady move like you did today. You'd better get home fast, Sebastian may be patient, but I guarantee you he's getting calls and texts from ladies that aren't so patient."

"I wouldn't want to put a cramp in his romantic life." Cassie grinned as she hurried toward the door. "Thanks again, Mirabel."

As Cassie hurried back toward the hardware store, where she'd parked her car, she realized that Trevor would be arriving with the statue fairly soon as well, and then Miles would show up to inspect it. Her casual day had become quite busy. She drove the short distance back to her house and spotted the blue pickup truck out front right away. It only took her a moment longer to spy the man leaning against a pillar of her front porch. Sunlight ignited the strands of blond hair that peeked out from beneath his baseball cap.

"The man even sparkles." Cassie rolled her eyes and laughed at herself as she stepped out of her car. Despite her certainty that she was first, not interested in a relationship, and second, far out of his age range, she couldn't deny the way her heartbeat quickened at the thought of being face to face with him. Surely, he would be annoyed. He had a right to be. He had offered to help her out, free of charge, and showed up when he said he would. She had almost completely forgotten about his generous offer and left him waiting, and that in itself made her cringe with regret. She wanted her life here to be different, she wanted to form trusting friendships, and a community, both of which she didn't feel she had in the city. But already she was off to a rough start. She took a breath as she moved in his direction. Hopefully, he would accept her apology, and they could start off on the right foot.

CHAPTER 6

As Cassie approached the front porch, Sebastian looked up at her from beneath the brim of his cap. His lips spread into a relaxed smile as he studied her. When he spoke, his voice was smooth.

"Do you keep all your men waiting, or just me?" Sebastian's eyes locked to hers. His dark brown eyes crinkled at the corners, as his smile spread even wider.

Stunned by Sebastian's question, and still a bit distracted by the voice he delivered it in, Cassie took a step back as she regarded him.

"I don't have any men." She cleared her throat as her heart pounded. "I mean, I don't keep anyone waiting." She sighed as her heartbeat quickened even more. "I mean, I know I kept you waiting, and I'm sorry that I did, but I don't usually."

"Alright." Sebastian straightened up, which positioned him closer to her, and pulled his cap off his head. "I guess I'll just have to take your word for that. But you must have had a better offer to forget about a plumbing problem."

"I did." Cassie walked up to the door to unlock it and put some distance between the two of them. The closer he stood, the faster her heart raced. "Not a better one, just a different one."

"Must be a fascinating fellow." Sebastian followed her into the house.

"Actually, a fascinating female." Cassie glanced over her shoulder as she smiled. "Mirabel offered me a job, and in all of the chaos of the lunch rush, I just completely forgot I was supposed to meet you. I do apologize. I really am not usually like this. Punctuality is important to me."

"Relax." Sebastian slid his hands into the pockets of his jeans as he continued to study her. "I had nowhere better to be."

Cassie settled her gaze on his and guessed that wasn't true. According to Mirabel, he had plenty of people willing to occupy his time.

"Thank you for waiting for me." She hesitated for

a moment as it dawned on her that they were together alone in her living room. In the city, she never would have invited a stranger, or a person she had met for only a few minutes, into her home. But she hadn't even thought twice about welcoming Sebastian.

"What's the problem?" Sebastian crossed the distance between them, his eyes still locked to hers.

"Sorry, it's just that I don't know you, and, I'm new to town, and well things are just happening so fast." Cassie sighed as she tried to get her heartbeat under control.

"Cassie." Sebastian spoke her name in a soft, calm tone. "I meant, what's the plumbing problem? If you're uncomfortable being alone with me, you can wait outside while I take a look." He held up his hands as he took a step back. "I know I would never do a thing to hurt you, but you can never be too careful."

Cassie's cheeks flushed as she realized that now she'd likely offended him twice.

"It's in the bathroom." She pointed to the still open bathroom door. "I turned the faucet on, and only sludge came out."

"I bet I can have it running clear for you in no

time." Sebastian turned and walked toward the bathroom.

Cassie followed after him, uncertain how to make up for their awkward conversation so far. Then she spotted her muddy sundress on the floor that she'd abandoned earlier in the day. "Sorry, I didn't have a chance to clean up." She snatched the dress up.

"Rolling in the mud already?" Sebastian quirked an eyebrow as he looked over at her and grinned. "I'm guessing there's a lot about you I don't know yet, Cassie."

"It's nothing like that." Cassie sighed as she gave up on trying to make a good impression. "I made a mess of things with my neighbor, Tessa. Her dog dug out from under her fence, then when I tried to put the dog back in, her goats got out, and I tried to catch them."

"Wow." Sebastian crouched down and pulled a few tools from the tool belt that hung around his waist. "It sounds like you had a rough start this morning. No one enjoys a run-in with Tessa."

"So I've heard." Cassie crossed her arms as she leaned back against the wall and watched him work. "Is she really that bad?"

"She can be." Sebastian reached around behind the clawfoot tub. "She has become a bit of a loner and presents a tough exterior. But if she is on your side she will do anything she can for you." He turned the faucet on, and water rushed from the faucet. "There you go."

Cassie's eyes widened as water began to fill the tub.

"Wow, you work miracles!"

"Nah, it's not a miracle." Sebastian grinned. "The water wasn't on. Now, you'll want to let it run for a bit to clear out the pipes. This place has been empty for a while. Once it runs clear, give it about another ten minutes, then you should be good to go."

"Seriously?" Cassie pressed her palm against her forehead as she closed her eyes. "You must think I'm pretty stupid not to figure that out."

"No." Sebastian stood up. "I would never think that." He looked into her eyes as she opened them. "I just think sometimes we get so caught up, so busy with life, we don't see what's right in front of us."

"So true." Cassie managed to mumble her words as she tried to ignore her racing heart.

"I'll be on my way then." Sebastian stepped past her, though his eyes remained on her. He stepped through the door of the bathroom.

Cassie took a breath and only then realized she'd been holding it.

"Unbelievable," she muttered under her breath. Her childish behavior made her wonder how she'd ever managed to handle anything on her own.

"What's that?" Sebastian paused at the front door and looked back at her.

"Your payment." Cassie cleared her throat as she walked up to him. "How much for your time? And please, charge me from the time you arrived."

"Oh well, it was a long wait." Sebastian ran his hand along the slight stubble that coated his jaw. "Let's see, I'd say dinner should cover it."

"What?" Cassie's hand froze in her purse.

"It's the way we do things around here." Sebastian shrugged as his charming smile returned. "Neighbors don't charge neighbors. But if you'd like to share a meal with me, well that would more than compensate me for my time."

Cassie narrowed her eyes as she wondered if she should play along.

"From what I hear, you've got plenty of people to share a meal with. How about I just write a check?" She pulled her checkbook out.

"Oh, is that so?" Sebastian's voice thickened just enough to indicate displeasure. "Already buying into the rumors, huh? I thought you would know better than that. It's alright, if you don't want to go to dinner, just say so. But if you're interested in having a friend here in Little Leaf Creek, I'd say take your time and get to know someone, don't just assume the rumors are true."

"I'm sorry." Cassie sighed as she gazed at him. "I feel like I've offended just about everyone since I've arrived here."

"I'm not offended." Sebastian placed his cap back on his head. "Feel free to call me if you have any more trouble, Cassie. I'll be happy to help."

As the door closed behind him, Cassie still wasn't sure how to take him. One second she was sure that he was teasing her, the next she wondered if she'd just misinterpreted his words. Had he really wanted to go to dinner with her? She couldn't imagine why. Either way, it was best that the dinner didn't happen.

CHAPTER 7

Cassie listened to the sound of the water running as she gazed into the mirror. Already, in just a few hours she had managed to make some friends, and maybe some enemies, offend a few people, and get a job that she hadn't expected to want. If her first day in Little Leaf Creek was any indication of what the rest of her life would be like there, she guessed she needed to be prepared for quite an adventure. She pulled her hair back into a loose ponytail and began to unpack the few boxes piled up in her room. She knew when the moving truck arrived the next day, she would have a lot more work to do.

As Cassie set one of her favorite books on the

built-in bookshelf beside the spot her bed would be, she heard a light knock on the front door. A quick glance at her phone revealed it was close to five. When she opened the door, she found Trevor on her porch.

"Hi Trevor." Cassie smiled at him. "Thanks so much for delivering."

"It's no problem." Trevor rocked back on his heels nervously, then met her eyes. "Are you sure about this? If you were just trying to be nice, you can tell me. I don't want you to get into trouble because of me."

"Trouble?" Cassie glanced past him at the statue that he'd carted into the center of her yard. "Why would I get into trouble for displaying your art?"

"I warned you about the historical society." Trevor glanced over his shoulder, then back at her. "They're not easy to deal with. I just don't want them to give you a hard time."

"I am certain that I can handle it." Cassie looked into his eyes. "Your art deserves to be on display, and I feel lucky to be someone who can say they own a piece of it. Now, about placement." She stepped past him and down the steps of the front porch. "I think here would be best." She pointed to a patch of worn grass near the center of the front yard. "That way the tree over there doesn't block any light from getting to it."

"That does seem like a good spot." Trevor followed after her, then began to move the statue into place. "I'll have to come by and see it all lit up by the sun."

"Please do. I'd love to get your opinion on the placement once we see what the sun can do." Cassie grinned as she looked around the statue at him. "I have a feeling Rainbow is the perfect name."

"Here, right?" Trevor eased the statue off the dolly.

"Yes, I think that's perfect." Cassie touched it lightly to test its stability. "I think it's pretty secure."

"Trust me, you don't want to bolt it down. You'll have to move it soon enough." Trevor's cheeks reddened as he glared down the street.

"Trevor, have you no faith in me?" Cassie smiled. "I told you, it's not going anywhere."

"And I tell you, unless you're trying to put in a fancy sports bar and have enough money to grease the palms of the right people, you're going to have a fight on your hands." Trevor frowned as he rounded his shoulders. "It's not that I don't have faith in you,

Cassie. It's just, I know this town, and you don't. The historical society only speaks one language, and it involves a lot of zeroes."

"Interesting." Cassie crossed her arms as she recalled the group she'd sat down to lunch with earlier in the day. "So, you don't think they care about the town at all?"

"Some of them do, I guess. But the ones that make the decisions, they can be bought. Otherwise, how could a bar that's been part of this town for over one hundred years, be completely renovated into a sports bar with giant televisions and speakers that can be heard throughout town?" Trevor raised his eyebrows. "Does that sound like historical preservation to you?"

"Not at all." Cassie pursed her lips at the thought. "You may be right, Trevor, I might have a fight on my hands. But that's okay with me. I've got a lot of fight in me, too, and plenty of time to defend what I believe in."

"We'll see." Trevor grinned, as he shook his head. "It's hard not to have faith in you, Cassie. You make me want to believe that you're the warrior you claim to be."

"Warrior," Cassie repeated the word as her lips

spread into a warm smile. "Yes, I like the sound of that." She thought about the many times she deferred to the preference of others. It was just easier that way. It was expected, in her role, as the CEO's wife. She had been successful as the manager of a small museum, but being the CEO's wife had always been her priority. But that was all behind her.

"Here's the rest." Cassie pulled out another two twenty dollar bills and held them out to him.

"No." Trevor took a step back, then shook his head. "I can't take any more money from you."

"What did I tell you about charging what it's worth? And what about delivery?" Cassie frowned as she studied him.

"Consider it the friends and family rate." Trevor's eyes shined as they met hers. "You've already given more than you can ever know, just with your kindness and support."

"Fine, fine, I'll just come by and buy more art." Cassie grinned as she watched him hurry down the sidewalk. It warmed her heart to think that he considered her a friend. Could it be the start of a genuine connection? He was young, but she was fine with having friends of all ages. Life didn't happen the same way at the same time for everyone.

Cassie decided the perfect way to enjoy the evening was with a cup of tea on the front porch with a perfect view of her new art. She rummaged under the sink in the kitchen and found an old teapot stowed there. After inspecting it for any signs of mold or critters, she cleaned it out, then filled it with water to boil. It was a relief to see the clean, crisp water flow, although it reminded her of how foolish she'd been not to know to turn the water on and let it run.

Sebastian.

Cassie's cheeks burned at the memory of him, his accent, his easy smile, the way his voice tensed when she mentioned his way with the ladies. She guessed there was a lot more to know about him than what was on the surface. She set the teapot on the stove and turned the burner on. As she dug through a small box she'd brought with her for the kitchen, she found her favorite peppermint vanilla tea. The flavor always put her at ease and cleared her mind. She pulled out her favorite mug, painted with images of her favorite sites from around the world, and set it on the counter.

As the teapot began to shriek, Cassie thought it sounded off. Louder than it should be, and oddly pitched. She frowned as she took it off the burner.

The sound of rumbling water silenced, but the shriek did not. She dropped the teapot on the stove as she realized the sound was coming from outside the house. It wasn't the shriek of a teapot, it was a scream, from a very real, and very frightened person.

CHAPTER 8

Cassie's heart lurched as the scream echoed through her senses. She ran for the front door and threw it open in time to see a crowd gathering in the dim evening light, right in front of her property.

Startled, and a little frightened, she eased her way down the front steps.

"What is it? What's happened?" Cassie noticed a woman in front of the statue she'd purchased, hunched over something on the ground.

"He's dead, he's definitely dead." The woman stumbled back a few steps.

Cassie braced herself for the sight, but nothing could prepare her for the shock as she peered around the statue and caught sight of a man on the ground. That dark hair, with silver streaks.

Cassie took a sharp breath as she realized it was Miles, the man she'd met earlier in the day, the man who had agreed to come by to help determine if she could keep her statue there.

Sirens shrieked through the commotion of the crowd that had grown even bigger within just a few seconds.

The woman looked at Cassie, her eyes wide.

"He's been stabbed."

"What?" Cassie stumbled back and pressed her hand against her stomach as it twisted with fear and shock. "But how?"

"Excuse me! Clear the area!" A stern voice barked as the crowd began to part.

Cassie caught sight of a man in a suit as he pushed his way through the large group, headed straight for her. Maybe it was his sharp gaze, or his muscular frame, or simply the badge that adorned his chest, but something about him made Cassie shudder and draw back.

"This can't be." Cassie's heart pounded as she looked back down at Miles on the ground. "This has to be some kind of nightmare."

Cassie looked back up at the man who stood in

front of her. The man's jet-black hair was cut neatly to frame his face, which only accentuated the symmetry of his high cheek bones and the strong slope of his nose. In another situation she might classify him as handsome, but in that moment, he reminded her of every billionaire she'd met or seen portrayed on television or in books. It was his air of arrogance, and authority, that made his eyes locking onto hers, send a shiver down her spine.

"Are you the property owner?"

"Yes." Cassie forced the word from between her lips.

He turned his attention to the woman who still stood beside Miles. "Are you alright, Shelby?"

"I'm not sure, Oliver." Shelby bit into her bottom lip and shook her head. "I saw him there, and I hoped that he was still alive, but he wasn't."

"Did you see anyone nearby? Anyone running off?" Oliver focused his attention on her.

"No one." Shelby shook her head again, then gasped. "Oh Ollie, how could this have happened?" She moaned and fell toward him.

Oliver quickly opened his arms to catch her.

Cassie's heart raced as she tried to piece together what might have happened. Could a man really be murdered on her front lawn without her hearing a single thing?

Cassie guessed he could be, since she hadn't heard Shelby's scream until she took the teapot off the burner.

"It's going to be okay, Shelby." Oliver straightened her up and looked into her eyes. "Go on over to Brenda, you'll be fine. I'll be over to talk to you soon, alright?"

Cassie felt some relief as she observed his compassionate nature. Perhaps he wasn't as rigid as her first impression of him had indicated.

Shaken, she took a slow breath in an attempt to calm herself.

As Shelby walked over to another woman in the crowd, Oliver turned to face Cassie.

"What exactly happened here?" Any trace of compassion had vanished from the steel-gray eyes that stared at her.

"I don't know. I was making tea." Cassie's voice sounded foreign to her, and eerily calm, despite the fact that panic ran wild through her.

"You were making tea?" Oliver narrowed his eyes.

"Miles, his name is Miles." Cassie took a step toward the body as her mind spun.

"Don't." Oliver stepped in front of her.

"I can't believe this happened." Cassie gasped as she tried to make sense of what she saw before her. "He was supposed to come over tonight."

"So, you knew he was here?" Oliver didn't move.

"No, I didn't know." Cassie shook her head. "He said he would come by in the evening. I didn't know he was here, not until I heard the screaming."

"Whose screaming?"

"Shelby's." Cassie shifted her gaze back to his. "I just moved here. Today. It's my first day."

"Quite a first day." Oliver's lips twisted into something between a grimace and a smile.

"What's going on out here?" A voice raised above the din of the crowd and the still blaring sirens.

Cassie turned to see Tessa just outside of her gate in a crisp white t-shirt and pristine blue jeans.

"This is none of your concern, Tessa." Oliver turned to face her as well.

"Oh, is that so, Detective Graham?" Tessa stepped through the gate. "Is that Miles?" Her voice wavered some.

"This is a crime scene, Tessa, you need to step away." Oliver left Cassie where she stood and stalked toward Tessa.

"A crime scene, huh? Are you sure he didn't just

keel over from being so uptight?" Tessa straightened her shoulders as Oliver stopped in front of her.

"Enough, Tessa." Oliver held up his hands. "He was murdered."

"Funny." Tessa smiled as she shook her head. "What really happened?"

"It's true. Now, please get out of my crime scene." Oliver pointed toward Tessa's house.

Cassie's thoughts raced as she tried to figure out what might have happened. Who would kill Miles? Who would murder him right on her property? How had she not heard it happen? Panic caused her senses to heighten as she listened to the snippets of conversation in the crowd. She easily felt the tension that vibrated between Tessa and Oliver.

"Alright then, I'll go." Tessa took a few steps back.

"And you." Oliver turned back to face Cassie. "You're going to need to come down to the station. I have some questions for you."

"To the station?" Cassie nodded, her hope for a peaceful cup of tea on the porch, now just a dream she'd had at some distant time.

"No, you don't." Tessa stepped back through the gate. "You don't go anywhere with him without a lawyer. Do you hear me, Cassie?"

Tessa's voice sounded distant as Cassie stared at

the detective in front of her. Somewhere in the back of her mind she recognized the shadow that darkened his eyes. Suspicion. It dawned on her that Detective Oliver Graham considered her a murder suspect.

"Tessa, I told you to stay out of this." Oliver growled.

Dazed, and completely confused, Cassie looked between Oliver and Tessa.

"I didn't do anything."

"Don't say a word, Cassie!" Tessa's harsh tone rattled her.

"I just have some questions, that's all." Oliver's voice grew smooth.

Cassie sensed the suspicion beneath it. She couldn't shake the memory of that shadow in his eyes. Of course, he would suspect her. She was new to town. She'd had plans to meet Miles. Why wouldn't he suspect her?

"But I didn't do anything." She tried to ignore the tears that started to form.

CHAPTER 9

"I just need to ask you some questions." Oliver's voice remained stern.

"Let her go, Ollie!" Tessa called out.

"It's a crime scene." Oliver gritted his teeth. "I can't let her go and you know that."

"Please." Cassie drew a sharp breath. "Please, just give me a moment to calm down." She felt some relief as Oliver relaxed his stance slightly, though he remained close enough to stop her from leaving.

"Can't you see all of this is a shock to her?" Tessa frowned as she stepped between them. "Give her a second to breathe."

"Or a second to get her story straight." Oliver stepped around Tessa to Cassie's side. "I need to speak with you right away. A man has been murdered on your property, do you understand that?"

Cassie clenched her jaw as he looked into her eyes.

"I understand." She noticed a glimmer in his eyes that lifted the shadow that darkened them, only for a moment.

"Will you cooperate and come down to the station?" Oliver tilted his head in the direction of a patrol car.

"I'll drive her." Tessa gently put her hand on Cassie's shoulder and steered her toward the gate. "I'll drive her down to the station, you're not going to put her in the back of a patrol car."

"Tessa." Oliver's tense voice rose slightly. "You shouldn't interfere."

"Someone has to." Tessa looked at Oliver, then guided Cassie through the front gate toward her house.

Cassie had no idea if she should go with her. But she did know that she didn't want to get into any police vehicle. She glanced back over her shoulder and found Oliver staring straight at her.

Panic filled her chest as she struggled to take a breath.

"Easy now." Tessa led her down her driveway to

an old jeep. "You've got to keep your wits about you, and that means you have to breathe."

"He thinks I did it." Cassie paused beside the passenger side of the jeep and looked into Tessa's eyes. "He thinks I murdered someone."

"He thinks everyone did it." Tessa jerked the door of the jeep open and waited for her to climb in. "He's a detective in a town where nothing ever happens, and he's just walked into a murder investigation. He has to investigate everyone."

Cassie settled into the passenger seat of the jeep and drew a deep breath.

"That doesn't make me feel any better."

"It shouldn't." Tessa slammed the door shut, then walked around to the driver's side. She opened the back door and Harry jumped onto the back seat. "Good boy."

As Tessa started the engine, she looked over at Cassie.

"Look, Oliver has a lot to prove, but he's a good detective. He's jumping the gun because he has to. In a town like this, rumors spread like wildfire, and sorting out the truth from the story, can make solving a crime very difficult. He's going to want as much information as he can get out of you as quickly as possible. All you have to do is say as little as possible, and make sure that everything you say is true."

"You said I should get a lawyer." Cassie stared at her house as the jeep rolled past it. The lights from the police car splashed across her brand new statue. It really did look like a rainbow. She noticed Trevor in the crowd, his head low, and his hands shoved deep into his pockets.

"Do you have a lawyer?" Tessa looked over at her.

"No." Cassie thought about all of the lawyers she used to know. The thought of calling any of them filled her with dread. She didn't want her old life seeping into her new one.

"Then you're going to have to either get one, or be smart enough to handle this yourself. Otherwise, Oliver is going to keep pestering you. Like I said, just say as little as possible, and make sure that everything you say to him is the truth. Oliver has a nose on him that can smell a lie a thousand miles away."

"You seem to know a lot about him." Cassie frowned as she looked over at Tessa.

"I should. I taught him everything he knows." Tessa jerked the jeep to the right as she turned down a side road.

"You're a police officer, too?" Cassie's eyes widened as she studied her.

"That's a story for another time. We need to focus on you right now." Tessa tipped her head toward a well-lit, large parking lot at the end of the road. "That's the police station, and once we're there, you're going to be on your own."

"Why are you helping me?" Cassie watched her as she pulled into the parking lot.

"That's not what you need to be concerned about." Tessa parked a few feet away from the front door. "Now, once Oliver gets you in an interrogation room, it's just going to be the two of you. Don't let his good looks fool you, he's a beast when he wants to get to the truth." She stared straight into her eyes. "Don't let him rattle you. Do you hear me?"

"I didn't do anything," Cassie repeated.

"I know you didn't." Tessa held her gaze for a long moment, then she reached across her and popped open the passenger door. "Go on, now. No tears, no sniffling, got it? Keep your wits about you."

Cassie stepped out of the jeep and swallowed back a sob that threatened to overtake her. She didn't want to go into the police station. She didn't want to see Oliver again. But she knew that she didn't have a choice. She did her best to take Tessa's advice, and struggled to get control over her emotions. Yes, it had been a terrible day. A day she never could have expected. A day that she wished she could start over, and perhaps never leave the house. But it wasn't nearly as bad as the day Miles had. She recalled their exchange at the diner, he'd been so full of life, and determination. Now, he was gone. Whatever she could do to help find his murderer, she would. Once Detective Graham saw that she wanted to be his ally, not his enemy, she was sure that shadow in his eyes would disappear.

As Cassie pulled open the door, she wondered what this would lead to. Would she step back through it again? Would she be charged with murder? Certainly, she hadn't committed the crime, but would her innocence be enough to keep her out of handcuffs?

CHAPTER 10

The police station was quieter than Cassie expected. Perhaps she had seen too many police shows, but there was no one bustling about, no crowd waiting to be seen. In fact, as she walked across the tile floor she wondered if there would even be anyone to greet her. Just as she was about to call out, a woman stepped through a door behind the front counter and set her eyes on Cassie.

"Can I help you, ma'am?" She straightened the badge on her uniform.

"Yes, I think so." Cassie walked up to the counter, then cleared her throat. "I'm here to speak with Detective Graham."

"Oh yes, Oliver told me that you'd be in." She

walked around the counter, then gestured for Cassie to follow her. "What a crazy mess, huh?" She led her down a short hallway and opened the first door on the right. "We don't get too many crimes around here."

"I guess that is a good thing." Cassie peered through the door at a wide open space. There was a desk on one side, with a well-cushioned desk chair behind it, against the wall to the left of it a large couch spread from corner to corner. In front of the desk were two wooden chairs, each lined with thick cushions.

"He asked that you wait here for him." The officer shrugged. "I'd make yourself comfortable, my guess is it'll be a little while before he comes in."

"Okay, thank you." Cassie watched as the woman walked away. She had expected an interrogation room with a metal table, and two folding chairs. Instead, she was surrounded by bookshelves, and photographs that hung on the walls. She glanced over his collection of books, impressed by some of the titles, curious about others. Her nerves began to settle as she thought she might have a few moments to calm down. A photograph on the wall caught her attention. It featured Oliver, with a woman who looked a lot like Tessa, both in police uniform. She moved closer to it for a better look.

"Take a seat."

Oliver's voice came from right behind her.

"Oh!" Cassie jumped back as she turned to face him.

"Wherever you like." The detective brushed past her and sat down behind his desk.

Cassie inched her way over to one of the chairs in front of his desk and sat down.

The detective's eyes focused on a file in his hand which he spread out across the desk in front of him.

"You just moved here?" The detective didn't look up.

"Today." Cassie sighed. "The moving van comes tomorrow."

"Today. But you bought a piece of artwork, created by this man?" The detective pushed a picture of Trevor in her direction.

"Yes, I did." Cassie noticed the picture appeared to be a mugshot.

"And you had lunch with Miles?" The detective looked up at her then, his expression stern.

"Yes, I did. At Mirabel's. Along with other members of the historical society." Cassie folded her hands in her lap.

"I see." The detective leaned back in his chair as he studied her. "And was this piece of artwork you purchased a subject of discussion at this lunch?"

Cassie hesitated. She knew it would be wiser to have a lawyer present, to say as little as possible, but she sensed that if she tried to evade any of his questions, he would only suspect her more.

"Yes. I was informed that the historical society probably would not approve of the art placed in my front yard. Miles offered to come over to have a look at it and decide what his recommendation would be as to whether it could be approved." Cassie met his eyes. "I didn't know he had arrived. I was making some tea."

"So, you're telling me that a man was stabbed to death on your front lawn and you didn't hear a thing? You didn't hear anyone arguing? You didn't hear anyone calling for help?" The detective tapped the picture in front of her. "Did you see him near your house?"

"I didn't hear anything, no. The teapot was loud, and when I took it off the stove, that's when I realized that there was something happening outside." Cassie looked down at Trevor's picture. "He delivered the artwork to me, but that was earlier in the evening."

"So, you didn't see him after that?" The detective lifted his eyebrows as he studied her.

Cassie recalled seeing Trevor in the crowd of people outside of her house. She didn't want to get the young man into trouble.

"No, I didn't." She looked down at her folded hands.

"I'm sorry?" The detective rested his elbows on the desk and leaned closer to her. "Are you saying you didn't see him again after he delivered the artwork?"

"I didn't see him again." Cassie tightened her lips as she looked up at him.

"Why would you do that?" The detective narrowed his eyes.

"Why would I do what?" Cassie held her breath.

"Lie to me?" The detective stood up from his chair.

Cassie's heart skipped a beat as she recalled Tessa's warning not to lie to Detective Graham. Could he really tell that she was?

The detective walked around the side of his desk, then leaned back against the corner of it as he gazed at her.

"Did you kill him, Cassie?"

"Of course not." Cassie glared at him. If he hadn't

been so close, she would have stood up and walked out of the office. To do so would have meant bumping into him on the way out.

"Then why did you lie to me?" He shook his head as he frowned. "Why are you hiding something from me?"

"Trevor had nothing to do with this. He's just a kid." Cassie looked back at the picture on the desk.

"Is that it? You're trying to protect him?" Oliver picked up the photograph and held it a few inches from her face. "This kid, that you think is so wonderful, has been in and out of jail since he was fifteen. He has a real problem with theft. In fact, most of that piece of art you purchased, was probably stolen. So, do you still want to protect him?"

"Look, Oliver, I know that I'm new here." Cassie sighed as she scooted her chair back a few inches to create some space between them.

"Detective Graham." He set the photograph back down on the desk.

"Detective Graham," Cassie repeated his name as she looked back at him. "I might not know all of the secrets of this town, but I do know innocence when I see it. Maybe Trevor has some problems, but he's not a killer."

"I hope he thinks the same thing about you, because I'll be talking to him next." The detective stood up from the edge of his desk and gestured to the door. "You can go now. But I'll be in touch."

"I'm sure you will be." Cassie glanced back at him briefly, before she continued out the door. There wasn't much chance of convincing him that she wasn't a suspect now. She'd lied to him, he knew it, and that would only make him more suspicious. Her skin crawled with frustration as she made her way out of the police station and back to the parking lot.

Headlights flashed in her direction, momentarily blinding her. She squinted through the bright light and spotted Tessa's jeep.

"How did it go?" Tessa looked over at Cassie as she climbed in beside her.

"Not well." Cassie frowned.

"You lied to him, didn't you?" Tessa started the engine.

"Not about anything important."

"That's the thing about Oliver. Everything is important to him." Tessa turned out of the parking lot of the police station. "Well, I guess this means we have our work cut out for us."

"What do you mean?" Cassie glanced at her.

"We're going to need to figure out who actually

killed Miles, before your new home ends up being behind bars."

CHAPTER 11

"Come in." Tessa held the front door open for Cassie, as Harry rushed toward the door. "Easy pup." She gave the dog a few solid pets. "Sorry, he's a bit of a jumper."

"I don't mind." Cassie grinned as she stroked the dog's fur.

Tessa led her into the kitchen. Cassie noticed that her place was a bit rundown, but neat and cozy.

Tessa walked to the sink and turned on the faucet to wash her hands.

"Have a seat." She tipped her head toward the small, square kitchen table. Cassie guessed that it couldn't seat more than two people. Which meant she didn't often have guests. As she settled in a chair,

Harry placed his front paws in her lap. She scratched his chin and stroked his ears.

"What did our local detective have to say?" Tessa dried her hands.

"He seems to think that Trevor was involved but I don't think he was." Cassie tried to slow the speed of her pounding heart. As much as she wanted to believe that there was a way to get out of all of this, the way Oliver had looked at her, left her with a strange sensation in the pit of her stomach.

"So, you really think the kid is innocent?" Tessa shooed Harry away from the table, then grabbed a bowl from the shelf above the sink. "Why?"

"I just do." Cassie sighed as she watched her set the bowl on the counter. "Sure, he may have gotten into a little bit of trouble, what kid doesn't? But that doesn't make him a killer."

"No, you're right, it doesn't." Tessa turned to face her. "But it doesn't make him innocent either. What did you lie about?"

"Detective Graham asked me if I had seen Trevor again after he delivered the statue to my house." Cassie sighed as she closed her eyes. "I just said that I didn't. I did see him in the crowd outside of my house after Miles was found, but so what? Most of the town was out there."

"If you didn't think it was a big deal, then why did you lie about seeing him?" Tessa popped open the cabinet beside her and pulled out a bag of flour.

"I don't know." Cassie opened her eyes again as Tessa measured off three cups of flour. "What are you doing?"

"Making a cake." Tessa walked over to the end of the kitchen bench and gathered a few items on top.

"A murder is nothing to celebrate." Cassie stared at her, puzzled.

"It's what I do." Tessa cracked an egg on the edge of another bowl. "It helps me to relax, and to think clearly. Isn't there anything that you do that helps you with that?"

"I make lists." Cassie pulled her notebook out of her purse. The first half was filled with lists about the move, from what to pack, to what restaurants to stop at on the drive, to all the phone calls she had to make to set up the utilities in her new home. She flipped to a blank page and jotted down a simple question.

Who killed Miles?

"That's one way to do it." Tessa flashed a grin at her. "I guess making a cake is kind of like making a list. I think about all of the most important ingredients, and make sure they're all mixed in. So, if we want to figure out who killed Miles, we need to find the right ingredients."

"Known enemies?" Cassie looked up at her as she tapped the end of her pen against her lips.

"Anyone that tried to paint their porch?" Tessa chuckled, then nodded. "That's a good place to start. But there are other factors, too." She began to mix the butter and sugar together. She raised her voice to be heard over the sound of the mixer. "There are things we know, that can help us. We know that he was stabbed. Which means that whoever killed him had to be close to him, and armed."

"Good point." Cassie jotted down the murder weapon. "What about the strength to kill him? Miles was short, but he would have fought back right?"

"That's a good point. Whoever did this managed to subdue and stab Miles, all without drawing the attention of anyone else. If the person caught him by surprise it would have been possible to stab him without using much strength." Tessa added the dry ingredients alternating with the buttermilk to the butter mixture. "Miles had made quite a few enemies over the years by denying projects. He had the ear of the right people on the committee, which led to him having the most influence."

"Trevor mentioned something about him

approving renovating the old bar in town into a sports bar. Something far more modern than people would expect here?" Cassie frowned. "Is it true that he would take bribes to approve projects?"

"If it was, I didn't know about it." Tessa poured the batter into the cake pans and put them in the oven. "But there are some things about this town that I don't know. I try to keep my nose out of everyone's business. Which is what you should have done."

"Are you saying all of this is my fault?" Cassie set down her pen. "How?"

"How?" Tessa put the bowls in the sink, then turned around to face her. "You managed to get to know a murder victim, one of his potential killers, and an obsessive police detective, all in just a few hours of being here. You brought this murder to your front yard, didn't you? What if you had just walked right past Trevor and his statue? What if you hadn't insisted on placing it in your front yard? What if you had never spoken to anyone on the historical society?"

Cassie's heart sank as she realized that Tessa might just be right. If buying the statue had been what triggered the murder, how could she not put some of the blame on herself?

"I just wanted to help a young artist." Cassie winced as she looked down at the list on her notepad.

"Cassie, you seem like a nice person." Tessa pulled a chair out from the table and sat down across from her. "But nice people, aren't very smart."

"What?" Cassie stared at her. "First you blame me for the murder, and now you're telling me I'm dumb?"

"Wait just a minute. I never blamed you for the murder." Tessa held up her hands. "The only person to blame for Miles' death is the person who killed him, which I am convinced is not you, otherwise you would not be in my kitchen right now. What I said was, you are to blame for putting yourself in the middle of it all. If you'd just kept to yourself, you'd be hearing the rumors and watching the crowds gather, and would not be the target of a police investigation."

"Maybe so." Cassie drew a slow breath then smiled. "But I guess I'm not the only dumb one here, since you seem to be right in the middle of it with me."

"I'll admit, it's not my smartest move. But I couldn't just stand by and watch as Oliver took you in for questioning." Tessa stood up to check the timer on the oven then wiped her weathered hands on a towel that hung on the oven door.

"I saw a picture of the two of you in his office." Cassie narrowed her eyes as she studied Tessa's expression. "How do you know him exactly? You said you taught him everything he knows. Did you work together?"

"How do we know anyone?" Tessa smiled.

"That's it?" Cassie sighed. "That's all I get? Some off-hand remark that's meant to keep me quiet?"

"How I know Oliver isn't important right now. You need to focus on yourself right now, not me." Tessa crossed her arms as she gazed at her. "I'm helping you because it seems like the right thing to do, and because you did your best to protect Harry, Billy and Gerry. But this is really your mess, not mine, and you need to focus on that and make sure it's fixed."

"You're right, I should go." Cassie stood up from the table. "It was nice of you to offer to help, Tessa."

"Sit down." Tessa pointed to her chair. "You haven't even had a slice of cake yet."

CHAPTER 12

Cassie stared hard at Tessa as a prickling of suspicion surfaced in her mind.

"Why do you really want to help me, Tessa? I think it's pretty clear from our first encounter, and from the things I've heard about you, that you prefer to keep to yourself. So, why are you being so nice to me?"

"Don't confuse my determination with kindness." Tessa added some butter to a bowl. "Why I want to help shouldn't be your concern. Just know that with me on your side, you're going to get through this."

Despite the fact that Cassie had no reason to believe her, the confidence she conveyed put her at ease. Maybe she just wanted to believe her. Maybe she wanted to think she had one friend looking out for her in a town that she felt had already begun to turn against her. She eased herself back down into the chair and looked at the bare tabletop. After the day she'd had, a piece of cake sounded good, and the smell that carried through the kitchen made her mouth water.

Tessa began beating together the butter, confectioners' sugar, milk and vanilla extract. When she stopped the mixer she looked over at Cassie.

"Tell me something, Cassie." Tessa grabbed a gallon of milk from the fridge and poured them each a glass. "Why did you come here?"

"Does it matter?" Cassie ran a fingertip along the condensation on the outside of the glass she handed her.

"It could." Tessa sat down across from her again.

"I'll answer one of your questions, if you answer one of mine." Cassie locked her eyes to Tessa's.

"Okay, that seems fair enough." Tessa folded her hands on the table. "So, answer."

"I needed a new start, a new beginning. I always did what was expected of me, I lived the life that people wanted me to, and now I want to figure out what I actually want. I thought this would be the place for me, but I guess I was wrong." Cassie sighed. "Does that answer your question?"

"Not all of it, but I'll take it." Tessa smiled. "It's a start."

"How do you know Oliver so well?" Cassie held her gaze.

"I already told you that's off limits." Tessa narrowed her eyes.

"You agreed to the terms." Cassie sat forward and continued to stare at her.

"Oliver and I have a history. That's all you need to know." Tessa knocked her hand lightly against the table. "It's not something that's up for discussion."

Cassie was about to argue the point, but the hardness in her eyes silenced her. Yes, she wanted to know more. But at the moment Tessa seemed to be the only person on her side. Did she want to change that?

"Tell me what you know about Miles." Cassie picked up her pen again. "Did he grow up here?"

"Yes." Tessa stood up and opened the oven. The kitchen filled with a sweet aroma.

"Oh, that smells so good." Cassie licked her lips.

"Just wait until you taste it." Tessa grinned. "But it has to cool first." She looked back at Cassie. "Miles and I grew up together, actually. He was always a nosy kid. He liked to be in charge of everything."

"I'm sorry, Tessa, I didn't even think about the

fact that you might be grieving over his loss." Cassie frowned. "I've been so focused on my problems, and I didn't even consider your grief."

"Enough of all that." Tessa waved her hand in the air. "Miles and I were not friends. We never were. We just happened to be in the same place quite often. It's hard not to be in a town as small as this. But after I left Little Leaf Creek we didn't speak, and that didn't change when I returned."

"Where did you go?" Cassie watched as she turned the cakes out of the pans and onto a cooling rack.

"You're asking the wrong questions again, Cassie." Tessa shook her head. "If it's enemies you're looking for, Miles had a long list. But there's a big difference between being angry and being a murderer. There aren't many people around here I'd pin down as capable of such a thing."

"But it had to be someone." Cassie tapped her pen on her notepad.

"Oliver gave you a good suspect. Trevor is known around town for his temper." Tessa put the pans in the sink. "Maybe Miles went to him first. Maybe he told Trevor that he wasn't going to allow the statue to stand in your front yard. Maybe Trevor got angry about it, snapped, and decided to get rid of Miles."

"I don't want to think that." Cassie pressed her fingertips against her forehead.

"Not wanting to think it, doesn't mean it isn't true. If you're going to get out of this mess, you've got to see clearly, and from all angles." Tessa began to spread a thin layer of frosting across the top of one of the cakes, then she placed the other cake on top and spread the frosting over the sides and top of the cake. "It's a bit soon to do this, but I think we could both use a slice, and then some rest." She cut two slices of the still slightly warm cake and set each one on a plate. She handed one over to Cassie, along with a fork. "Not a word about calories either, or I'll never let you set foot in this house again."

Cassie couldn't help but smile as she picked up her fork.

"Thank you."

"I hope you enjoy it." Tessa sat down with her own slice.

"I mean, thank you for all of this." Cassie looked across the table at her. "I don't know how I would have handled all of this on my own."

"You're stronger than you think, Cassie." Tessa dug her fork into the slice of cake. "Now eat."

Cassie took a bite of the cake and let it melt against her tongue. She could taste the delicious vanilla buttercream frosting and moist cake. It was sweet, but not too sweet.

"This is just magical."

"Magical." Tessa grinned. "I don't think I've heard that one before."

"Are you a baker?" Cassie recalled the picture of her in Oliver's office. She was in a police uniform. "Did you become one after you left the force?"

"Eat your cake, Cassie." Tessa picked up her glass of milk and took a big swallow.

Cassie took another bite and did her best to silence her curiosity.

"You said that Miles might have enemies going back years, but what if this was a new person that came into his life? I wonder what was really going on with the renovations on the old bar. Trevor said Miles was going to make it happen, even though the rest of the historical society was against it. Maybe they were in daily contact about it. The owner of the bar might know something more about who had a problem with Miles." She finished off the last bite of her cake, then took the last sip of her milk.

"That's an idea." Tessa nodded. "Though I'm not sure that he'll talk to you."

"It's worth a try." Cassie carried her plate and glass to the sink. "I'm going to get some rest." She turned back to face her. "You're right, Tessa, I am stronger than I think. I'm certainly not going to let any small town detective try to run my life."

"That's the spirit!" Tessa smiled. "I knew you had it in you."

Cassie stared at her a moment longer. Had she known? Or was there another reason that Tessa had decided to get so involved with her? She and Detective Graham had obviously been close at some point. Maybe they still were. As she left Tessa's house, she did her best to ignore her own suspicions. Like it or not, she was all she had.

CHAPTER 13

After a fitful night's sleep on the blow-up mattress she'd toted with her in her car, Cassie woke up with a sense of determination. Tessa was right, she needed to clear her name so she could enjoy her new life in Little Leaf Creek.

Cassie turned on her shower and smiled with relief at the clear water that flowed out.

"Thank you, Sebastian." She let the water run over her fingertips as she tested the temperature. While she waited for it to warm up, she brushed her teeth and spent a few moments gazing at her own reflection. The day before she was new in town. Now, she was a murder suspect. The easiest way to clear her name was for the real murderer to be caught.

After a quick shower, Cassie headed out in the direction of town. She didn't know exactly where the sports bar was, but it didn't take her long to spot it. The outside looked as if it was being prepared for a facelift, and the sign that hung above the one-story building stood out due to its bright and flashy imagery. The rest of the shops had small signs in uniform colors. Yes, the owner of this establishment definitely wasn't following the rules of Little Leaf Creek.

Cassie parked and walked up to the front door. Although the sign in the window said coming soon, she noticed lights on and movement inside. After a light knock, a man came to the door. He looked to be about the same age as Miles and Tessa, perhaps nearing his sixties. When he opened the door, he smiled at her.

"Ah, the famous new face. I'm sorry I can't offer you a drink, no liquor license yet, but you can come in if you'd like." He stepped aside to allow her inside.

"Thanks." Cassie followed him in. "Nice place, I've heard a lot about it already."

"Oh, I'm sure." He rolled his eyes. "You'd think I was setting fire to the whole town just because I want to replace the bricks with some siding. There goes Fred Meyers, ready to destroy all of Little Leaf Creek."

"I hear you're fairly new to town, too." Cassie sat down on one of the bar stools as she smiled at him.

"Not new exactly." Fred leaned against the bar. "I grew up around here, but I moved away for about fifteen years. Now, I'm back, ready to open my business."

"I grew up in a small town, too, and headed for the city the first chance I got." Cassie glanced around at the large screen televisions mounted on the walls. "It looks like you've made quite a lot of progress. When are you opening up?"

"Actually, that's up in the air at the moment." Fred frowned as he looked toward the front windows. "I have quite a battle with the historical society facing me, now. If they don't approve the changes, the town council won't give the go-ahead."

"Really?" Cassie shifted on the stool as she focused her attention on him. "But it looks like you're all set up to open. Didn't you know about the historical society before you set all of this up?"

"I knew about it, sure. But Miles had assured me that he would be able to get the approval of the committee. With no Miles, I doubt my chances are too good with the rest of the society." Fred sighed as he stood up. "I guess, I might have to kiss my dream of bringing this backwards town into modern times, goodbye."

"But Miles couldn't have convinced all of them on his own. I'm sure you have some other supporters on the society." Cassie took a sip of her water. "Maybe there's still a chance."

"I guess I'll just have to wait and see. They should be deciding soon, but my guess is, Miles' death will delay it a bit." Fred's jaw tensed.

"I'm so sorry for your loss. You two must have been close." Cassie frowned as she looked into his eyes.

"You could say that." Fred sighed. "I still can't believe it happened. He was such an energetic person. You could hear him coming from miles away with that laugh. But now, he's just gone." He snapped his fingers. "I'm not sure how that happens really."

"I don't think any of us are." Cassie clenched her jaw as she held back a swell of emotions related to her own loss. "Good luck with your bar."

"Thank you. Maybe when I open up, you can come in for a drink." Fred nodded to her, then turned back to the boxes stacked behind the bar.

As Cassie let herself out through the front door,

she recalled the snap of his fingers. He claimed that he was sad about his friend's death, but she didn't see sorrow in his eyes when he spoke about Miles. She saw something different. Anger? Frustration?

Cassie took a few minutes to walk around the outside of the bar. She snapped a few pictures of the changes that Fred had already made to the building. It stuck out in her mind that Miles had been so certain he could convince the rest of the society to recommend approval of Fred's project to the town council. Why had Miles been so confident? It seemed to her that the people that had shared a table with her at the diner the day before, had no intention of approving anything like that. What did he know, that made his view of things so different?

With this thought still stuck in Cassie's mind she made her way toward the diner. She hoped that Mirabel would still have her, with all of the rumors flying around town about her involvement in Miles' murder.

Cassie pushed the door open and spotted Mirabel wiping down one of the tables close to the front window.

"Hi Mirabel." Cassie inched her way inside and braced herself for Mirabel's disapproval.

"Cassie." Mirabel smiled as she walked over to the front counter. "I was hoping to see you today."

"You were?" Cassie followed after her.

"I heard about your rough night." Mirabel handed over Cassie's apron. "I wasn't sure if you'd be in today or not."

"I thought I'd come in and see about my schedule." Cassie looped the apron over her head. "Unless you don't want to employ a murder suspect."

"Don't be ridiculous." Mirabel rolled her eyes. "I'm not judgmental, as long as you don't kill any customers, you're welcome to work here."

"Great." A laugh bubbled past Cassie's lips.

"I knew I could cheer you up." Mirabel tossed a stack of menus down in front of her. "We're about to get hit with the lunch rush, so be ready. We don't have a hostess and we're down one busboy."

"Sounds like it's going to be busy." Cassie turned toward the front door just as a rush of people began to pile through. By the time she had a chance to catch her breath, she'd handed out all of the menus in her hands. When the door swung open again, she scrambled behind the counter to get more. After she seated the trio of women who had brought along their knitting, she caught sight of Rose and Charles on their way into the diner.

Cassie's heart fluttered. If Detective Graham suspected her of murder, would Rose and Charles suspect the same thing?

CHAPTER 14

"Maybe you should take their table." Cassie looked from Rose and Charles to Mirabel. "I'm sure I'm the last person they want to see today."

"Go on." Mirabel tipped her head in the direction of the table that Rose and Charles chose. "You're going to have to face them sometime, it might as well be now."

Cassie drew a breath and looked back at the table. Rose gave her a short wave, while Charles kept his nose buried in the menu he held. Mirabel was right, she would have to face them sooner or later, she just wished that it wasn't sooner. As she walked over to them, she tried to remind herself that she had nothing to feel guilty about. She had no involvement in Miles' death, and even though a part of her suspected that if she had never set certain things into motion the day before, Miles might still be alive, she had no way to prove that.

"Good afternoon Rose, Charles." Cassie paused beside the table. "I'm so sorry for your loss. I wish I'd had the chance to get to know Miles a little better."

"Do you now?" Rose stared straight at her. "From what I've heard, you were pretty upset at the idea of him not approving the artwork that you purchased."

"We never even spoke about it after we all had lunch together." Cassie pulled a notepad out of the pocket on her apron. "Can I take your order?"

"You didn't speak to him at all yesterday evening?" Charles closed his menu and set it on the table in front of him. "But we both know that he went to your house. He told us that he was on his way."

"Yes, he came to my house, but I had no idea he was there, until he was already dead." Cassie frowned as she twisted the pen she held between two fingers. "Even if he had rejected my plans, I wouldn't have been angry. I would have figured something else out. Things like that just don't get to me."

"Aren't you perfect?" Charles glared at her. "I'll

tell you what we know, Cassie. We know that our friend left to go to your house, and a short time later wound up dead. So, you can tell us that you're sorry for our loss as much as you want, but forgive me if I'm not too quick to believe you."

"Charles." Rose placed her hand over his and looked into his eyes. "Now, think of your heart. You can't get upset like this."

"I'm sorry, if you want someone else to serve you, I'll see what I can do." Cassie started to step away from the table as tears of frustration burned in her eyes.

"Wait a minute, dear." Rose caught her hand by the wrist and pulled her back. "Charles is just upset. This is quite a shock to both of us. Of course, we would never want anything to happen to Miles, but for him to be murdered." She took a sharp breath. "It's just such a tragedy."

"It is." Cassie tapped her pen against the pad. "I just wish that I could have done something. Maybe if I had realized what was happening outside, I could have helped him."

"Or you could have put yourself in danger, too." Rose shook her head. "Listen, we'll each take a special, alright?"

"You've got it." Cassie started to turn back toward

the kitchen. "I'll have it up for you as quickly as possible."

Even as Cassie walked away, she could feel Charles' hard gaze on her. She doubted that he shared his wife's sentiment about her. After handing their order over to Frankie, she checked on the customers at the counter. While taking their orders she heard two men chatting at one end of the counter.

"My point is, Miles was killed right next to her house. Everyone's trying to pin it on the new gal in town, but let's be clear, there's already someone in Little Leaf Creek that we can blame for Miles' murder."

Cassie glanced over at the two men and noticed that they huddled close together. One kept his ball cap tucked tightly onto the top of his head, the other had thick, brown hair and a broad smile.

"Tessa?" The other man shook his head. "She may keep to herself, and sure, she may be a little crazy, but that doesn't mean that she killed anyone."

"But it means that she might have." The first man leaned closer. "Are we all just going to pretend that she's not top on our list of people that could have done this?"

Cassie took a step back from the counter as the

other man's eyes fixed on her. Did he know she was the 'new gal in town' and on the list of people who could have killed Miles? She was an outsider, easily targeted, but Tessa? Was it just mean-spirited gossip, or was there something more to her new friend that everyone else knew, but she had yet to discover?

As Cassie turned in a few more orders, her cell phone buzzed in her pocket. She pulled it out to find a text from Detective Graham requesting her presence. She frowned as she wondered whether to return it. He'd asked her to meet him at a scenic overlook about fifteen minutes away but offered no explanation as to why. It struck her as odd, but at the same time she knew if she resisted, he would classify her as uncooperative.

"It's getting pretty quiet in here." Mirabel walked up to her. "If you want, you can head out and come back around dinner. Unless you need the tips?"

"No, it's alright." Cassie managed a small smile. She didn't want to let on that working at Mirabel's was just a way for her to integrate with the community, not a necessity, at least not yet. She had quite a comfortable cushion. "I'll be back around five?"

"Make it four-thirty, we get a lot of early bird

diners." Mirabel winked at her. "Great job by the way, I really appreciate your help."

"I appreciate you hiring me." Cassie took off her apron and hung it on a peg just inside the kitchen. She spared one more glance in the direction of Rose and Charles' table, then headed out the door. As she walked to her car, she sent a text back to Detective Graham to let him know she was on her way. Maybe if she asked the right questions, she could find out a little more about Tessa, their past relationship, and why some people in town seemed to think she was capable of murder.

Cassie entered the address the detective gave her into her phone and followed the directions the GPS offered. It led her to a highway, that didn't look anything like a highway. It was two lanes, and wound around a series of hills, with the creek following the same path. When she pulled off onto the overlook, she noticed Detective Graham's car parked alongside the guardrail that outlined the large semi-circle of space. She parked behind it. Her heart fluttered. Had he found something that made him suspect her even more?

Cassie started to open her car door, but he stepped up beside it before she could. He pulled the door open, his gray eyes already locked to hers.

"I have a question for you."

"Okay." Cassie stared up at him, still seated in her car, and braced herself for the question. After the last time he sniffed out her lie, she guessed telling the truth would be the best bet.

"Tell me, what made you move here out of the blue like you did?" Oliver continued to hold the door for her.

"I needed a change." Cassie forced a smile. "End of one story, the start of another." She stepped out of the car and hoped to break his focus on her as she walked over to the railing. "I had no idea it was so beautiful here."

"Thanks for meeting me." Oliver paused beside the guardrail and looked out over the side at the water that streamed past. "I know it was an unusual request."

"Anything I can do to help with the investigation, I'm happy to do." Cassie tried to meet his eyes as he continued to look down at the water. "You believe that, don't you?"

"I believe that you are trying to cooperate." Oliver finally looked up at her, his eyes heavy as they settled on hers. "But I've discovered some things about you that leave me a little unsettled."

CHAPTER 15

"Oh?" Cassie braced herself as she wondered what skeletons Oliver might have uncovered.

"You never told me that you are a widow." Oliver narrowed his eyes.

"You never asked." Cassie shrugged as she took a step back. Her heart pounded. He had been looking into her. He had been digging, and now, things she wasn't ready to talk about were going to be brought out into the open.

"It's usually information that people are pretty forthcoming about. I did ask what made you move here, and you left that part out." Oliver shook his head. "Which makes me wonder why. Why would you withhold that kind of information?"

"It's not a title I like to use." Cassie pursed her lips. "Is that such a terrible thing?"

"Running from the past, tells me you have something to hide." Oliver curled his hands around the metal guardrail as he continued to study her. "It tells me that maybe you have a guilty conscience."

"I'm not running." Cassie struggled to keep her voice even as anger spiked within her. "Did it ever occur to you that maybe I'm grieving?"

"I'm sure you are." Oliver's voice softened as he released the guardrail and took a step closer to her. "You went from glitz and glam, from luxury, to this?" He gestured to the woods that surrounded them and the creek beneath them.

"I chose to come here. I didn't choose to lose my husband." Cassie swallowed back a sob as tears filled her eyes. "I don't want to talk about this. Why is it even relevant?"

"I'm just trying to find out what happened." The detective took another step toward her. "You show up here, and a man ends up dead, you have to know how that looks."

"Yes, I know exactly how it looks!" Cassie took a step back. "It looks like the police around here don't know how to do their job, so they're trying to pin the whole thing on an outsider! It looks like their best detective is someone who will go after the easiest target he can find!"

Cassie's eyes widened at her words and she detected a flash of something in his gaze that made her wonder if she was safe on a ridge, in the middle of nowhere, alone with him. She backed away farther as her heart raced.

"I'm sorry, I shouldn't have said that."

"Miles was here." The detective ignored her words and looked straight into her eyes. "He was here on this ridge meeting someone, not long before he was killed. Was it you?" The sky darkened above them and rumbled around his words, making them feel even more ominous.

"It wasn't me, of course it wasn't me." Cassie shook her head. "Why don't you look a little closer at the people in your town instead of me? And to answer the question that you implied with all of this, no Detective Graham, I did not kill my husband." She turned on her heel and stalked over to her car.

"Cassie, I'm not done speaking to you!" His voice was full of authority.

Cassie didn't think that the badge meant she had to stay. She knew her rights well enough to know that she could walk away or drive away. She opened her car door and slid inside. She closed it just before he could reach it. She looked through the raindrop-splattered windshield at him as she reversed out of the overlook and back onto the quiet highway. She'd tried to cooperate, she'd tried to convince him that she could be an ally not an enemy, but he had upset her. Maybe she was being too sensitive but he had taken things too far by bringing up events that were still painful for her.

As Cassie drove back toward town, a part of her expected him to follow. She felt some relief when he didn't. But moments later a pickup truck pulled off a side road, and began to match her speed which was a bit higher than the posted limit.

Cassie glanced in her rearview mirror as the truck drew closer to her car. Despite the rain, she thought it looked a lot like Sebastian's truck. Was he trying to catch up with her? She stepped on the gas. She didn't feel like speaking to him. She wanted to be alone after her conversation with Detective Graham. Her focus on the road ahead of her increased, as the raindrops grew more frequent. She increased the speed of her windshield wipers. When she glanced in her rearview mirror again, she noticed that the truck had indeed caught up. In fact, it was tailing her so closely that she guessed if she slammed on her brakes it would cause quite an accident.

Cassie stepped on the gas again, but the slippery road beneath her tires made her think twice about it. She slowed down and hoped that he would pass her, so that she could go at the speed she preferred and could stay safe. However, the truck didn't pass her. In fact, it backed off a little. Seconds later it sped up to the point that she could hear its engine roar. It swept around the side of her car, then pressed in on it, as they neared a curve in the road.

Cassie tried to grip the wheel tighter, but the car was already sliding out of her control. She had pressed hard on the brake, which caused it to careen closer to the edge of the road. She felt her tires slip in the fresh mud and the car swerved toward the side of the hill. It slid to a stop just before it would have collided with the barriers.

Shaken by the experience and jarred by the seat belt that pinned her hard against her seat, she took a few breaths in an attempt to calm down. As it dawned on her that the person in the truck had forced her off the road intentionally, she looked wildly around for the driver. Would he try to finish the job by attacking her directly? When she looked at the road, she didn't see any other vehicles. There didn't appear to be anyone nearby, though it was hard to see through the rain that had begun coming down in sheets.

Cassie fumbled with her seat belt and managed to free it. Seconds later, she heard a car door slam. Her breath caught in her throat. Was this it? Was the person going to try kill her again? She popped her door open and tried to jump out of her car. Her legs wobbled, as she was still stunned from the near crash. Her shoes slid in the mud, which sent her sprawling across the ground.

"Cassie!" A familiar voice called out to her. That accent. She knew exactly who it belonged to. Her heart pounded as she struggled to get to her feet.

"No don't!" Cassie shrieked as she felt his hand curl around her wrist.

"Cassie, it's okay, it's me, Sebastian." He tightened his grasp on her hand. "Did you have an accident?"

"It was you!" Cassie brushed her rain-soaked hair from her eyes and glared up at him.

"What?" Sebastian pulled her to her feet as his gaze roamed her body from head to toe. "Are you hurt? I have an ambulance on the way."

"Why? Why would you call an ambulance when you were the one who ran me off the road?" Cassie pulled away from his touch.

CHAPTER 16

"Cassie, you're confused." Sebastian stared into her eyes. "I didn't run you off the road. I just saw your car on the side of the road and stopped to help."

"No, that's not true." Cassie backed away from him as she heard the sound of an ambulance approaching. She heard another sound from not so far away, the sound of a police siren. Her stomach twisted as she realized that it must be coming from Detective Graham's car. "I saw you, I saw your truck behind me!" She tried to slow her breathing as her heart pounded.

"Cassie, I don't know what you saw, but it wasn't me." Sebastian gently curled his hands around her arms just above her elbows. "Did someone do this to you? Did someone run you off the road?"

"Let go." Cassie took a step back as he released her. Detective Graham's car pulled onto the shoulder, his headlights bright in the rain that had begun to ease.

"What's going on here? I heard an emergency call over the radio." Detective Graham jogged toward them.

"Someone ran me off the road." Cassie winced as she realized that she had no way to prove that. Sebastian claimed that he had arrived later. "Someone in a truck, just like his." She peered through the rain at the other vehicle on the side of the road. Instead of the blue pickup truck that she had seen Sebastian drive before, it looked like an old station wagon.

"Just like his?" Oliver turned his attention on Sebastian.

"My truck is in the shop." Sebastian held up his hands. "I don't know what Cassie saw, but it wasn't me, and it wasn't my truck."

"Are you sure there was a truck?" Oliver turned back to face her.

"Yes, of course, I'm sure." Cassie's thoughts spun with the revelation that Sebastian's truck was in the shop. If it wasn't him that ran her off the road, then who was it, and why?

"Did you get a look at the driver?" Oliver squinted up at the few raindrops that still fell. "Even a glimpse?"

"No." Cassie sighed. "The rain was heavy, and the headlights blinded me when he drove up behind me." She frowned as she looked over at her car. "I thought he was going to slam right into me."

"You keep saying he." Oliver moved closer to her, his eyes narrowed. "Are you sure you didn't get a look at the driver?"

"No, I didn't. I saw the truck, and it looked like Sebastian's truck, so I guess I just assumed he was driving it." Cassie glanced over at Sebastian, who continued to stare at her, his jaw tight.

"But it wasn't me. You believe me, don't you?" Sebastian tried to meet her eyes.

"I don't know what to believe. I just want to go home." Cassie's stomach lurched as she realized that she had good reason to be at home. The moving truck was due to deliver all of her possessions in less than an hour. "I have to go."

"Wait a minute." Oliver stepped in front of her. "You should get checked out, in case you're hurt."

"I can't be hurt." Cassie frowned. "The truck

never hit me, and I didn't hit anything with my car. I'm fine. I have to go." She started to step around him.

"Don't you want to fill out a report about this?" Oliver stepped in front of her again. "If you don't file a report, I can't investigate it."

"Would you, even if I did?" Cassie glanced back at him. "I'm pretty sure you've already decided a few things about me, and I doubt that you have any interest in helping me out."

"That's not true." Oliver crossed his arms and watched as she started off toward her car again. "I do my job, Cassie, nothing more, and never anything less."

"Then you figure out who ran me off the road." Cassie stared back at him as the panic of the incident rushed through her once more. She believed as her car slid through the mud that the person in the truck wanted to kill her. She couldn't shake that sensation or the fear that it brought with it. Meanwhile, the one person in Little Leaf Creek that was supposed to help her, preferred to argue with her. And why wouldn't he, when he thought she was a murderer? "Let me know when you do."

"Cassie, why don't you let me give you a ride home?" Sebastian stepped forward, his expression tense with apparent concern. "You shouldn't drive after something like this."

"No, thank you." Cassie glanced at him for a moment. He claimed he wasn't the one who ran her off the road, but she wasn't sure if she should believe him. She wasn't sure of anything anymore. Maybe her big move, her new life, had been a huge mistake. She settled in her car and turned the engine on. A part of her expected Detective Graham to stop her, even to arrest her, but instead both men watched as she pulled back onto the road and drove back in the direction of town. As she gripped the steering wheel, she realized that Sebastian was right. Her entire body trembled. She hadn't felt this frightened since the doctor stepped through those double doors with a look on his face that told her everything he didn't want to put into words.

Cassie slowed down as she passed the sports bar in the middle of town. She spotted Fred in the alley beside the bar. He was shaking his head and pacing up and down the alley. He seemed agitated. Was he waiting for someone? Cassie wanted to watch him to see what would happen next. But at the moment she needed to get back to her house and deal with the moving truck that had likely already arrived.

Cassie was almost to her house when she spotted

Trevor hard at work in the same alley that she had seen him creating his art the first time. The piece was smaller with more rounded edges and a few different shades of metal intertwined. As he wielded the blow torch, she noticed the ripple of his muscular arms. She hadn't paid much attention to his physical stature the first time they'd met, but now it stood out to her. Having strength would have made it easy to subdue and kill Miles quietly, strength that Trevor clearly had.

A sharp and sudden fear snapped through Cassie as she wondered if she could be wrong. She'd insisted on Trevor's innocence, had she been distracted by his youth and his talent? She tried to imagine the murder playing out on her front lawn. Had Miles already spoken to Trevor? Had he told him that he intended to reject the artwork? Had Trevor been insulted? Had Trevor lost his temper? After killing Miles had Trevor taken a second to admire his artwork before he ran off? It seemed like a stretch to her, but it was possible that Trevor had killed Miles.

CHAPTER 17

Cassie parked along the road in front of the house. The large moving truck was already backed up in the driveway. The driver walked around the side of the truck and nodded to her. She noticed him stare at the mud on her.

"We've been waiting for you. I didn't know if you wanted us to start unloading. But we don't go into anyone's house without permission, even if they leave the door unlocked." He frowned.

"I didn't leave the door unlocked." Cassie looked up at the house and tried to recall the moment she'd locked the front door. She knew that she'd done it. She always locked the door when she left her house. It wasn't something that she thought about. It was automatic. Even though the house was new to her, she would have locked the door.

"It was unlocked when we got here. I went up and knocked on the door, and the door started to swing open." The driver shook his head. "I didn't go inside, though."

"Something's not right. Let me take a look." Cassie started up the driveway toward the front porch.

"Do you think someone was in there?" The driver followed after her. "You shouldn't go in there alone."

"I'm sure it's nothing. Let me just make sure that everything is as it should be." Cassie pushed the front door open. It was unlocked as the driver had claimed. But was he just saying that to cover up for letting himself in? She didn't think it would benefit him in any way to do so. Was it possible that she had left it unlocked?

Cassie made her way through the living room. Everything appeared to be in place, not that there was really anything to move around, since just about everything she owned was outside on the truck. As she stepped into the kitchen, she noticed a piece of paper on the counter. Her heart fluttered as she was certain it hadn't been there when she left that morning. She walked up to it, her heartbeat quickening as she saw the cursive letters scrawled across the paper.

"Today was a warning, if you don't back off, tomorrow won't be." Cassie's voice shook as she spoke the words out loud. She could only assume that the note referred to the near-accident. Whoever had been driving the pickup truck had also left her a note, inside of her house.

Cassie took a sharp breath as she heard footsteps on the front porch. When she reached the front door she saw Sebastian at the top of the steps.

"What are you doing here?"

"I want to talk to you." Sebastian remained at the edge of the porch, though his eyes locked to hers. "About earlier."

"I don't have time, I've already made them late." Cassie gestured to the men who stood behind Sebastian. "They need to unload the truck."

"We'll get started." The driver walked toward his truck.

Cassie turned back toward the house. Her mind was on the note. She had to figure out who had left it there. If someone had been able to get into her home that meant she wasn't safe there, and neither was anyone else.

"Cassie." Sebastian followed her to the door but

didn't step through it. "I don't know what's going on with you, but something is clearly wrong, I can see it in your face. It is not just about the accident today, is it? Has something else happened?"

"Sebastian, I'm sorry about today." Cassie turned to face him. "I must have been wrong about who was following me. But I can't talk about it right now."

"Cassie!" Sebastian followed after her. "Listen, I know you don't know me well, but I think I've been pretty kind since you've arrived. I can tell something is very wrong, not just the accident. Why don't you just tell me what else is going on so I can help you figure it out?"

"Is everything okay, Cassie?" Tessa's voice came from behind them. "Is Sebastian bothering you?"

"I'm trying to help." Sebastian turned toward Tessa. "I'm just trying to get her to listen to me."

"And she obviously doesn't want to!" Tessa shook her head.

"Stop!" Cassie looked out at them both. "I want to be left alone, please."

"You may want to be left alone, but that's not going to stop whoever ran you off the road today from doing it again, and succeeding the next time!" Sebastian looked straight into Cassie's eyes. "Do you want to be alone when that happens again?"

Cassie's heart fluttered with fear as she recalled what the note said. Next time, it wouldn't be a warning. Would she have survived it if the person after her had decided to kill her?

"What is he talking about?" Tessa turned her focus on Cassie. "Did someone try to run you off the road?"

"Yes, someone did." Cassie gazed at Sebastian for a long moment. A small part of her still believed that it was him behind the wheel. But maybe this was a chance to find out for sure if he knew about all of this, and the threatening note in her kitchen.

Both people on her porch had access to some degree to her home. Sebastian had been in it to fix the problem with the plumbing. Tessa had lived beside it long enough and she imagined she would know how to get in undetected if she wanted to. Either of them could have left the note if they really wanted to.

"Fine, you can both come inside." Cassie stepped away from the door, though her heart pounded with uncertainty, and watched them as they walked inside. She studied their expressions, she searched for any hint of deceit. If one of them had left the note, they would know what to expect, and their reaction might be different. When it came to having enemies, knowing the person's identity would be her best defense.

CHAPTER 18

*C*assie led the way into the kitchen without saying a word about what they might find there. She turned back and watched Tessa and Sebastian as they stepped inside. Tessa walked over to the counter first, her eyes settled on the note, but she didn't get close enough to read it.

"So, what exactly is going on here?" Tessa turned to face her and crossed her arms as she looked at her. "Are you going to fill me in?"

"I was driving back into town, and someone in a blue pickup truck ran me off the road." Cassie looked between Tessa and Sebastian. Each wore an expression of concern.

"Are you sure about that? Some of these people

around here just don't know how to drive." Tessa shook her head.

"I'm sure." Cassie looked straight at Tessa. "Someone wanted to get a clear message to me, and just in case I missed it, they let themselves into my house and left this." She gestured to the note on the counter. Again, she watched their reactions.

"Someone broke in?" Sebastian's shoulders straightened, his eyes narrowed, and his hands flew out of his pockets as he looked at the note. "What does it say?"

"Someone's really trying to scare you, huh?" Tessa peered at the note. She skimmed over it, then looked up at Cassie. "And you have no idea who?" Her tone remained calm.

If Tessa was concerned, she didn't show it. She just continued to gaze into Cassie's eyes.

"I have no idea who." Cassie shook her head.

Sebastian leaned against the counter as he read over the note.

"You need to call Oliver about this." He looked up at her, his eyes narrowed. "This is serious."

"I don't want to call him." Cassie frowned as she gazed at the piece of paper. "He thinks I killed Miles."

"He's investigating a murder. He thinks everyone

is a suspect." Sebastian sighed as he took a few steps closer to her. "I'm not the great detective's biggest fan, he's too serious for me, but he seems to give people a fair shake. You should talk to him about this."

"I'm not going to." Cassie shook her head. "I should just throw it out." She reached for the paper, but he caught her hand before she could grab it.

"Don't do that." Sebastian released her hand quickly and took a step back. "Keep it around. If something else happens, you might need it to prove that this has happened before."

"I think it's pretty clear that whoever is doing this, had something to do with Miles' murder." Cassie took a step back from the paper. "What I don't understand is why they're coming after me. I have nothing to do with any of it."

"Did you do anything that would make someone think that you're onto them?" Tessa peered down at the letter. "It sounds like you spooked someone."

"All I did was talk to the owner of the bar in town. I talked a bit with Mirabel and, Rose and Charles, this morning about it, too. But that's it." Cassie shrugged as she looked at Tessa. "I don't see why that would upset anyone."

"Maybe you stumbled across something you're

not aware of, and someone thinks you know more than you do." Tessa nodded. "I agree with Sebastian, I think you need to tell Oliver about this note."

"Alright, I'll text a picture of the note to Detective Graham. But I'm not going to speak with him about it. I can't stand being around him." Cassie took a deep breath.

"Interesting." Tessa looked at her, then turned her attention back to Sebastian. "Alright, let's help these guys out so that they aren't delayed even more."

Cassie opened her mouth to protest but decided against it. She felt bad about being late and she wanted to help them make up time if she could. She took a picture of the note, then sent it along with a short text to Detective Graham. She knew he wouldn't let it rest at that, but she hoped that she could avoid a face to face conversation.

After Cassie sent the text, she joined the four of them at the truck. She started helping them unload and showed them where the heavy items should go. The rest of the stuff was piled up in the living room.

Cassie was surprised at how strong and fit Tessa was even though she favored one leg. She easily navigated the steps with heavy items and didn't stop for a minute.

Soon, the truck was unloaded and everything was inside the house.

"All finished." The driver smiled as he walked over to her. "I just need your signature." He held out his clipboard to her.

"Thank you." Cassie signed the paper, then handed the clipboard back to him. She reached into her purse and pulled some cash from her wallet and handed it to the driver. "I'm sorry I was late."

"No problem. Thanks for this." The driver smiled and headed toward the truck. He handed over half the money to his assistant.

"Thank you." The assistant called out to Cassie and they hopped into the truck.

Cassie stepped back onto her porch where Sebastian and Tessa stood.

"I can help you sort out the furniture and boxes, so they're in the right spot." Sebastian looked at Cassie. "Most of the stuff hasn't been organized."

"I can handle it on my own." Cassie took a step toward the front door. "Thank you for your help."

"You can get it done a lot faster with extra hands." Sebastian shrugged as he met her eyes. "I'm glad to help."

"Thanks, but you've done enough." Cassie looked over at Tessa. "You both have."

"You heard the lady." Tessa nodded as she gestured for Sebastian to leave. "Let's let her have her peace."

Sebastian stared at Cassie a moment longer, then stepped off the porch.

"Thank you." Cassie called out to them.

As soon as Cassie stepped inside, she turned the lock and leaned her head against the door. She needed to catch her breath. The day had been overwhelming to say the least.

Her cell phone rang with the alarm she'd set to remind her of her evening shift at the diner. She didn't realize how late it was and shuddered at the thought of being surrounded by people, any of whom could have been the driver of the pickup truck that ran her off the road. But she guessed that it would be safer than being alone in her home. And maybe she would find a clue as to who it was.

After having a quick shower and changing her muddy clothes, she locked up the house, then headed to the diner.

As Cassie stepped inside the familiar setting, Mirabel's warm smile offered comfort to the chaos in her mind.

"I'm so glad you're here." Mirabel wrapped her arms around her in a loose hug.

Cassie's heart warmed as she returned the hug but held it for a few seconds longer than Mirabel intended. When she realized that she'd begun to cling to the woman, she pulled back and turned her attention to the apron that hung on a hook behind the counter.

"Do you know of anyone else that drives a truck like Sebastian's?" Cassie looped the apron over the top of her head, then tied it around her waist.

"A few people. Blue pickup trucks are the go-to vehicle around here." Mirabel grinned, then her jovial expression faded. "Cassie, is everything okay? You look so frightened."

"I'm just a little worn out." Cassie wiped her hand across her face. "It's been a very strange day."

"Do you want to tell me about it?" Mirabel looked into her eyes. "I can be a great listener."

"Maybe later." Cassie pointed out several cars that pulled into the parking lot. "It looks like the rush is starting."

"Okay later. Rose left a tip with a note specifically for you yesterday. I left it in an envelope in the back for you." Mirabel waved to a customer who walked through the door. "Brace yourself, honey, you're about to get introduced to Little Leaf Creek high society, at least they think they are." Mirabel gave a short laugh as she tipped her head toward a crowd of people headed through the door of the diner.

"Oh boy, I'll do my best." Cassie soon lost herself in the process of greeting and seating several of the people who came in. After a whirlwind of introductions, she managed to take over a dozen orders and pass them over to Frankie in the kitchen. It wasn't until then that she had a second to check her phone. Her heart dropped when she saw that she had several missed calls from Detective Graham, as well as two texts that indicated he was not happy with her lack of response. She glanced up from her phone in time to see the detective himself step through the door of the diner.

CHAPTER 19

Cassie ducked into the kitchen before Detective Graham could catch sight of her. She doubted he was there for a hot meal. The tension and scrutiny in his expression indicated that he was on a mission.

"Hey, if you're going to be in here, then you're going to put some plates together." Frankie pointed her in the direction of a few dishes that were ready to go. Cassie put together the orders, then piled the plates onto a serving tray. She stared at the door that led into the dining room and wondered if the detective might still be out there. He didn't seem like the type to give up easily. Had he asked Mirabel about her? She doubted that Mirabel would lie, she had no reason to.

"Don't let that food get cold, or I'm the one that has to hear about it!" Frankie banged his spoon against the side of the large pot of soup he'd been stirring.

Cassie jumped at the sharp sound, then nodded and flashed him a brief smile. From what she could tell he was a funny and nice guy, but he seemed to take his job very seriously. She tightened her muscles and forced her way through the door. Even if the detective was still there, she didn't have to talk to him. She didn't have to do anything, other than deliver food to waiting customers.

As the kitchen door swung shut behind Cassie, she spotted the detective at the front counter. His eyes locked on to her easily, as if he had been watching for her to come out of the kitchen. She looked away and pretended not to notice him as she began serving each of the waiting tables. She noticed a few more diners had been seated and were likely waiting to place their orders.

As soon as Cassie's tray was empty, she grabbed up a half-empty bottle of mustard and hurried toward the prep station to fill it. The second she stopped in front of it, she heard his voice beside her.

"Cassie, I've been trying to reach you."

"I'm pretty swamped." Cassie gripped the bottle

of mustard in her hand as tight as she could. She reminded herself that she needed to remain calm, especially around Detective Graham.

"Too swamped to discuss a threat against your life?" The detective sought her eyes even as she tried to avoid his.

"I sent you the text because I thought it might help in the murder investigation. I can take care of myself." Cassie felt the glass mustard bottle slip in her hand. Was she sweating that much? What was it about this man that left her on edge, but also oddly intrigued? In the same moment she didn't want to be anywhere near him, and also didn't want him to leave.

"Or you could let me do my job." Oliver took the mustard bottle from her hand and set it down on the table beside them. "It's my job to protect you."

"And also suspect me?" Cassie's gaze sharpened as she locked it to his. Her heart slammed against her chest. Was that hurt she felt surfacing within her? What sense did that make?

"Yes." The detective's voice hardened for a moment, then he shook his head. "You want me to find out who killed Miles, don't you?"

"Yes." Cassie took a step back as frustration washed over her and threatened to raise her voice.

"But I also want you to believe me when I tell you that it wasn't me. How can you expect me to think that you can protect me, when every time you look at me, all you see is a murderer? Why would you want to protect a murderer?"

"That's not what I see." The detective drew a short breath, then looked away from her. "It's what I'm supposed to see. Until I prove otherwise. But it's not what I see." When he looked back at her, his eyes seemed to brighten.

"Detective Graham, there are more important things that you could be doing right now." Cassie did her best not to think about what he'd just said. It wasn't so much the words he'd spoken, as it was the way he said them, labored and reluctant, as if he was confessing to something.

"It's Oliver, okay?" The detective glanced at the crowd of diners, then looked back at her. "I can see you are busy, but I'd really like to discuss this with you. I'm concerned about you being in that house alone after this. Is there anyone that can stay with you?"

"I'm brand new to town, but you already know that." Cassie smiled at a customer. "I don't know anyone here. But I'll be fine. I always am."

"Will you at least give me permission to go

inspect your locks, your doors, and windows? I'd like to see if there are any signs of someone breaking in." Oliver pulled his phone out of his pocket and checked a message before looking back up at her. "For my peace of mind?"

"I guess you're concerned you'll lose your prime suspect?" Cassie rolled her eyes, then stepped away from the counter.

"Cassie, do I have your permission or not?" Oliver stepped in front of her before she could get too far.

Cassie paused and looked straight into his eyes. Yet again she felt that strange push and pull, a mixture of dislike and attraction that left her more confused than ever. "Why do I get the feeling that it wouldn't matter if I gave you permission?"

"Do I have it or not?" Oliver continued to stare into her eyes and showed no sign of willingness to give in.

"Fine, if it will get you out of my way so that I can do my job, then go have a look. In fact, search the whole place while you're at it. That's what you really want, isn't it?" Cassie brushed past him and walked over to the table that needed her attention. Her skin prickled at the thought of him digging through her house. Why had she said that? Why had she invited him to investigate her even more? What if he did find a knife that he claimed to be the murder weapon?

Cassie turned back toward him and caught sight of him halfway out the door. It was too late to call him back. And what would he think if she did? Would he wonder if she had something to hide?

Stuck in what felt like an impossible situation, she focused her thoughts on the customers in front of her.

By the end of the dinner rush, her feet ached, and she remembered just how much work being a waitress could be. Many years ago, Michael had taken her away from that life, and now here she was, right back in it. Had she lost her mind?

She'd almost forgotten about Detective Graham, or Oliver, as he asked her to call him, when her cell phone buzzed with a text.

"I'm still at the house, I want to show you something when you're done." Cassie read the words out loud and felt her heartbeat quicken. There it was, a telltale sign of her getting far too invested in what the local detective thought about her.

"Anything I can help with in the kitchen?" Cassie walked past Mirabel.

"You're asking for more work after that crazy

shift?" Mirabel shook her head as she grinned. "If only I could clone a few of you I might get a few days off."

"I don't mind. I like to keep myself busy." Cassie glanced at her phone as she tucked it into her pocket.

"Or are you trying to avoid something?" Mirabel pursed her lips as she studied her expression. "Oh yes, that's it. You're trying to hide out here, huh?"

"Not exactly." Cassie shifted from one sore foot to the other. "I just don't know if I'm ready to go home yet."

"I know you've had a rough time here already. I just want you to know that you have a friend here." Mirabel took her hand and gave it a gentle squeeze. "I'm here if you want to talk. If someone is giving you a hard time, just tell me. I've known most of these people my entire life, I can help you navigate their quirky ways."

"Even Detective Graham? Can you help me navigate him?" Cassie looked up and met her eyes.

"Oh, Ollie?" Mirabel laughed and shook her head. "He looks like a tough cookie, doesn't he? He loves to wield that authority. But I'll be straight with you, Cassie, you couldn't have a better person on your side than him. He's loyal, he will investigate a crime no matter how long it takes, and he's genuinely dedicated to justice."

"And what if he's not on your side?" Cassie frowned as her phone buzzed again. "What if you're the one he's investigating?"

"Nothing to it, as long as you've got nothing to hide." Mirabel tilted her head to the side as she peered into Cassie's eyes. "Do you have something to hide?"

"Not anything that has to do with murder. I guess I just didn't expect to be turned inside out on my first full day here. When he looks at me, it feels as if he wants to know everything about me, from my middle name, to my shoe size." Cassie lowered her voice to a whisper as a few customers walked past. "Is he like that with everyone or am I just being sensitive?"

"From the way I saw him looking at you earlier tonight, I'd say that you've caught his attention in a way that most people don't." Mirabel released her hand and glanced toward the register. "I have to get to closing up. But if you're worried about Ollie framing you for something you didn't do, don't be. He would do anything to prevent an innocent person being accused of something they didn't do."

"Thanks Mirabel." Cassie sighed as she looked

toward the door. It didn't matter how long she put it off, he would still be there waiting for her when she arrived at home. Because he was that kind of a detective. The kind of detective that she would want on her side, if he was on her side. But he wasn't.

CHAPTER 20

On the short drive home, Cassie tried to talk herself into a calmer state.

"He's just doing his job. You need to let him. Keep it short, and get him out of your house." Cassie looked at her own reflection in the rearview mirror. "You are an innocent person, whether he knows that or not."

Cassie parked in front of the house, behind Oliver's car. Movement on the front porch indicated that he was there, though the lack of a porch light made it hard to distinguish exactly who it was. She glanced over at Tessa's house and saw that her porch light was on, as were many other lights in her house. She was tempted to invite her over, to be a barrier between herself and Oliver, but she didn't know whether she could completely trust her. She stepped out of the car and walked up to the front porch.

"Cassie." Oliver paused near the edge of the porch. "You must be exhausted."

The statement took her by surprise. Of all the things she expected from Oliver, empathy was not one of them.

"Maybe we can make this quick?" Cassie forced herself to meet his eyes, despite the fact that it was the last thing that she wanted to do.

"Sure." Oliver pulled out his phone. "I didn't find any evidence of forced entry, but I did find this." He pulled a picture up on his phone. "See those holes in the soil near the back door?"

"They're tiny." Cassie leaned closer to have a better look.

"Heels." Oliver pointed to the picture. "That's what I'm thinking. Was anyone around your property today in high heels?"

"Not that I saw." Cassie frowned as she gazed at the picture. "Could they be from yesterday? I did have heels on when I first arrived and I walked through the backyard."

"It's possible, but with all the rain we got earlier today, I'd assume those marks would have washed away. These look fresh to me." Oliver looked up from the phone. "Are you sure you didn't notice a woman around your house?"

"No, only Tessa. But I've never seen her wearing heels."

"It's a rare occurrence." Oliver smiled slightly.

"Even if there was another woman, how would she have gotten in? I locked all the doors." Cassie sighed as she looked up at the house.

"Are you sure about that?" Oliver tucked his phone back into his pocket.

"Yes, I'm sure. I've lived in the city long enough to always double-check my locks." Cassie walked up to the front door of the house.

"I'm only asking because when I arrived, the door was unlocked." Oliver followed after her as she stepped through the door.

"It was? Again?" Cassie's thoughts spun. "Was there a new note?"

"Not that I saw, but I didn't look around too much. I just came in long enough to make sure no one was inside." The detective paused near the door. "Contrary to what you may think, I have no interest in invading your privacy, Cassie. Things are always chaotic during a move, are you sure that you didn't leave the door unlocked?"

Cassie closed her eyes and tried to recall the act of locking the door before she went to the diner.

"I'm sure I locked it, but I can't actually remember." She shook her head as she sank down into a dining room chair that had yet to be moved into the dining room. "I don't usually make mistakes like that."

"Cassie, you've had a lot going on." Oliver pulled another of the chairs over beside her and sat down in it. "Did you give anyone else a key to the house?"

"The keys." Cassie's eyes widened as she took a sharp breath. "I can't believe I've been this stupid!" She shot up from the chair.

"What is it?" Oliver stood up as well and followed her as she walked over to a kitchen drawer.

"The realtor who sold me the house assured me that she changed the locks so that I wouldn't have to worry about it. I even paid extra for the service." Cassie took out an envelope and pulled out the keys. She held them up. "She had three extra keys made for me."

"But there are only two on that ring." The detective took the keys from her hand. "Who has been in your home?"

"Just Tessa, and Sebastian. But the note was left before Tessa came inside, so it couldn't have been her." Cassie's heart skipped a beat as she realized that Sebastian could have easily taken a key when she wasn't looking.

"Sebastian, who you think ran you off the road today?" The detective fiddled with the keys in his hands. "Why was he in your house?" His tone sharpened.

"He helped me with an issue I had with the plumbing. He offered to help when I went looking for a recommendation for a plumber at the hardware store." Cassie recalled the first moment that she'd met Sebastian, and the warm smile on his lips.

"That's pretty convenient." Oliver narrowed his eyes. "And you just let a complete stranger into your house?"

"Everyone is a stranger here!" Cassie took a step back as she crossed her arms.

"I'm sorry, you're right." Oliver held up one hand. "I didn't mean to insult you. If someone has a key to your home, then you'll need to change your locks right away."

"Yes, I'll go to the hardware store right now." Cassie grabbed her purse.

"Don't bother." Oliver shook his head. "It'll be closed. Things close up early around here."

"Then I'll drive to the next town." Cassie rubbed her hands along her arms. "I certainly won't be able to sleep tonight knowing that someone has a key to my home, someone that at least wants to scare me and possibly wants to hurt me, and probably killed Miles."

"Maybe you could get a room for the night." Oliver rubbed his hand along the back of his neck. "There aren't many towns around here that have stores open late. And for that matter there aren't many places to stay."

"Then what do you suggest?" Cassie began to pace. "Maybe I'll just stay up all night?"

"I could stay." Oliver cleared his throat.

"What?" Cassie peered at him, uncertain of what he meant.

"If you want, I could stay tonight. You'd be safe with me here. If anyone tried to get in, I would stop them." Oliver glanced toward the door.

"You would do that? You would stay here?" Cassie shook her head as she narrowed her eyes. "Why?"

"I told you, Cassie. It's my job to protect you. I take my job very seriously." Oliver glanced at the couch pushed against the wall in the living room. "I'll be fine on the couch. It'll be good for both of us.

It's probably my best chance to find out if anyone is stalking you. I can keep an eye out for movement outside."

"I don't think it's a good idea." Cassie crossed her arms to hide a faint shiver. "I'll be fine."

"Either, I'll be out front in my car keeping an eye on you, or in here. It's up to you." Oliver walked toward the front door.

"You can't sit out in your car all night." Cassie sighed as she let her arms fall back to her sides.

"I've done it plenty of times." Oliver turned to look at her, his tone a bit colder. "If you don't trust that I'm here to keep you safe, then me being here isn't a good idea, you're right."

"You're as much of a stranger to me as anyone else. Why should I trust you?" Cassie noticed the light on Tessa's front porch turned out, then looked back at Oliver.

"It's my job to find the truth, Cassie, not to cause harm. If you want me to find the truth, then you have to give me the opportunity to do that. It's pretty clear that whoever was involved in Miles' murder has decided to focus in on you. Do you really think you'd be safer without me here?" Oliver looked through the front window of her house. "This is a quiet town, but yesterday all of that changed. I don't know why, or who changed it." He looked back at her. "But you can trust that I have every intention of finding out."

"And I'm just supposed to accept that I'm no longer your main suspect?" Cassie met his eyes as he walked toward her.

"In a case with so little physical evidence I have to rely on motive, and proximity to guide my suspicions. You are a good candidate for both of those, don't you think?" Oliver tilted his head some and continued to hold her gaze. "You were on the same property at the time of the murder. You invited the victim here. Him being silenced could benefit you in some small way." He shrugged. "Would you think I was a decent detective if I didn't suspect you?"

As his words sunk in, she realized that he was right. She was as good a suspect as any, better in fact, than most. As the new arrival in town she garnered even more suspicion.

"That doesn't make it feel any better."

"I'm sure none of this does. So, if I stay you can get some rest, which will help you to feel better." Oliver pulled out his phone and scrolled through some texts. "You decide, I have to make a call." He stepped into the kitchen as he put his phone to his ear.

Cassie had no idea what to choose, when a knock on the front door distracted her. She peered through the window beside the door and saw Tessa on the other side.

CHAPTER 21

As Cassie opened the door, Tessa looked past her. "Is Oliver in there?"

"Yes, he is." Cassie gestured for her to step inside.

"I saw his car, and just wanted to make sure he wasn't up to something he shouldn't be." Tessa's eyes narrowed. "What is he doing, searching your property?"

"I told him he could have a look to see if he could figure out how someone might have gotten into the house to leave the note." Cassie watched her closely as she looked toward the kitchen in response to the sound of Oliver's voice on the phone. "You didn't notice anyone hanging around, did you?"

"I wasn't home most of the afternoon. I went to

talk to Karen and Avery. They didn't have much to offer. I then went to see Rose and Charles. I found them at their son's shop gossiping to anyone that would listen. I don't know how Bob can concentrate on fixing those cars with his parents in his ear all the time." Tessa looked back at Cassie. "Anyway, I wanted to get a feel of what the town is thinking about this whole situation, and those two are always in the middle of everything."

"And?" Cassie's eyes widened. "Did they have anything to say?"

"Only that they had lunch with you and Miles, as well as a few other members of the historical society just hours before Miles' death. Rose also mentioned that you left the table the first chance you had, and she felt that Miles had made you very uncomfortable." Tessa shook her head. "None of that sounds good for you."

"That's not what happened. Mirabel offered me a job and I decided to take her up on it." Cassie shrugged as Oliver walked back into the living room.

"But you don't need a job, do you?" Oliver paused beside her. "I've seen your financial records."

"Well, then you can answer your own question, can't you?" Cassie cut her eyes in his direction, unable to disguise her annoyance at his invasion of her privacy. "But money isn't the only reason people take jobs. I wanted a chance to get to know the community better, and I thought it would be a great opportunity for me. I can't just sit around."

"Makes sense to me." Tessa focused on Oliver. "What are you doing here?"

"I could ask you the same question." Oliver crossed his arms as he moved closer to Tessa. "I hear you've taken quite an interest in our newcomer."

"Someone has to help her. She's all alone here. Someone has to protect her." Tessa crossed her arms as well and stared right back at Oliver.

"You mean that someone has to protect her from me?" Oliver's tone sharpened.

"Take it easy. I didn't say that." Tessa let her arms fall back to her sides. "I didn't ask to be caught in the middle of all of this, and neither did she. If you spent less time questioning innocent people, you would have already solved this murder."

"Really?" Oliver smiled slightly. "So, tell me who did it? With all of your experience and expertise, you should already have it figured out, shouldn't you?"

"If you really wanted my help, you would have asked for it." Tessa took a slight step forward.

"You're right, I would have." Oliver nodded. "I

have this under control. I am just trying to help her. I think you should leave."

"Say no more." Tessa glanced over at Cassie, nodded to her, then walked out the door.

Cassie watched her go and wondered if she should call her back. But the fact that her place had been broken into made her hesitate. If Oliver had a problem with Tessa, maybe she should, too.

"Okay, if you want to stay, then you have to do something for me." Cassie turned to face him.

"What's that?" Oliver's expression remained tense.

"Tell me the truth about what happened between you and Tessa. I saw the picture of you together in your office. I know that you have a history." Cassie narrowed her eyes as he shook his head and turned away. "You tell me that I can trust you, but you're not willing to share anything with me."

"Is that what you want?" Oliver turned back to face her. "A peek inside my head?"

"I don't think it's too much to ask."

"Fine." Oliver ran his hand back through his hair as he sank down on the couch. "I grew up in Little Leaf Creek. Tessa was a local cop and when—" He cleared his throat.

"When?" Cassie took a step toward him.

"Something happened and she moved a few towns over." Oliver looked at his hands then back at Cassie.

"What happened?" Cassie's eyes widened.

"It doesn't matter, you'll have to ask her that. Anyway, I wanted to be just like her. I wanted to be a cop." Oliver looked up at her as she sat down beside him. "I moved away from Little Leaf Creek when I graduated from high school, so I could go to the academy and I got a job in the same police department as her. I then moved to another jurisdiction nearby and I came back here a few years later. When she retired, she moved back here as well."

"It sounds like you two must have been very close." Cassie frowned as she wondered what made Tessa leave Little Leaf Creek. "What happened between you two?"

"We have two different ways of policing." Oliver spread his hands out before him and stared at them, as if he might find some kind of answer in the pattern of lines on his palms. "We had a few clashes, and then one particularly big one." He looked over at her and frowned. "It's been tense between us ever since."

"That doesn't exactly explain what happened." Cassie looked into his eyes.

"I said, I'd let you take a peek." Oliver clasped his hands together as he studied her. "Isn't that enough?"

"I'm trying to figure out if I should trust her, Oliver." Cassie looked back toward the front door. "I just need to know what I'm dealing with. If she would do something that crossed the line—"

"No." Oliver took a sharp breath as he looked away from her. "No, she would never do anything like that." He stood up from the couch and began to pace the length of the living room. His watchful gaze lingered on the front window. "I don't think she would have broken in here. I have no idea why she would do something like that."

"But you don't know for sure?" Cassie stood up as he paced back toward her.

"It's been a long time since we've been close. I can't say for certain that she didn't do it, but I can say that if she did, it probably wasn't to hurt you. She seems to care about you. Which says a lot." Oliver paused in front of her. "There are a lot of people that I suspect of things in this town, but Tessa is not one of them. Although, I do have to investigate everyone."

Cassie nodded as she stared at him. His words didn't make her feel any calmer. If anything, they indicated that there was something more she should know about Tessa. Why did she leave Little Leaf Creek? What had caused their clash? Should she trust that Oliver wanted to protect her, or did she need to question whether it was more important to him to protect Tessa?

"I'll get us some coffee." Cassie headed into the kitchen to get a break from the strange tension that filled her whenever she was near Oliver. After the coffee was brewed, she returned with a mug for each of them.

"You should try to get some rest." Oliver took her mug of coffee from her and set it on the table in front of the couch. "This isn't going to help with that."

"I think I can decide when I should and shouldn't have coffee." Cassie picked up the mug and carried it to her room. Just when she thought she might begin to understand Oliver, he did something to annoy her. His controlling tendencies reminded her of the life she'd left behind, a life she never wanted to be caught up in again. She turned the lock on her door and sat on the edge of her bed. Reluctantly, she set the coffee mug down on her bedside table and decided not to drink it. She did need a good night's sleep, though she wasn't sure if she could get that with a stranger in her living room.

A few minutes after resting her head on the pillow she drifted off.

CHAPTER 22

Cassie jolted awake hours later, to the smell of fresh coffee. She had a quick shower and slipped on some fresh clothes, then stepped into the kitchen to find Oliver pouring coffee into a mug.

"Here." He held it out to her without meeting her eyes.

"Thanks." Cassie took the mug and blew across the surface of the coffee. "I guess all was quiet last night?"

"Completely." Oliver nodded. "I guess whoever threatened you thought you got the message."

"Maybe." Cassie recalled Tessa's visit the night before. Now that she knew that Oliver was on the case, she might have decided to back off. She grabbed her keys and purse. "I have to go to work."

"Okay then." Oliver swallowed the remaining coffee in his mug, then set it in the sink. "Let me clean up here."

"Don't worry about it, I'll get it later." Cassie walked toward the door, then paused and turned back to face him. "Oliver, thanks for staying last night."

"Just doing my job." Oliver walked past her and out through the front door.

As Cassie watched his car pull away, she felt unsettled. Was he annoyed that she had pushed him out the door so early? Was he suspicious that there had never been a threat in the first place? It was hard for her to figure out what he might be thinking.

On her drive to the diner, Cassie couldn't get thoughts of Tessa out of her mind. She'd been kind to her, but why had she been kind to her? Was she trying to be her friend, or was she trying to find her way into her house? She tried to picture her as the killer.

Cassie parked in front of the diner. She took a sharp breath as she realized that Tessa could really be the killer. She was nearby, it sounded as if she had a bone or two to pick with Miles, she could have taken the opportunity to kill Miles. But a few annoyances in the past didn't really amount to a motive, did it?

As Cassie walked into the diner, she placed a call to the hardware store to order new locks. Once she'd done so, she tucked her phone into her pocket and walked up to the front counter.

"Good morning, Mirabel." Cassie walked around the end of the counter and set her purse on a shelf as she reached for her apron.

"Good morning?" Mirabel crossed her arms and smiled. "Is that all you have to say to me?"

"Uh, yes?" Cassie looped the apron over her head and narrowed her eyes. "Am I missing something?"

"Oh honey, this whole town knows what happened last night." Mirabel raised her eyebrows. "Are you really going to hold out on me?"

"I'm not sure what you're talking about." Cassie tied her apron around her waist.

"Don't play innocent with me." Mirabel picked up a pot of coffee and carried it over to an empty mug at the end of the counter. "His car was parked out front all night."

"Oliver? Are you talking about Oliver?" Cassie sighed as she watched Mirabel fill the mug with coffee. "That was just business. Someone managed to get into my house and leave a threatening note, then I noticed that one of my keys to the house is missing. Since it was too late for me to change the locks, he offered to stay to ensure my safety." She frowned as she stared at the mug of coffee. "Who is that for?"

"One of our regulars, he's always the first customer in, and I make sure his coffee is ready for him." Mirabel looked into Cassie's eyes. "Are you really telling me that nothing happened between the two of you?"

"Mirabel, the last thing on my mind is romance." Cassie swept her hair back into a ponytail. "Did you miss the part about the threatening note? Someone is after me."

"You poor thing." Mirabel pursed her lips as she shook her head. "You've been through it, and you've barely moved in. I promise, things are going to get better from here."

"Unfortunately, I don't think it's going to get better unless I can figure out who took my key." Cassie ran her hand along her forehead.

"What about Trevor? Not that I really think he would ever murder someone." Mirabel set out sugar and cream for the unclaimed coffee.

"Trevor hasn't been in my house." Cassie looked out through the front window of the diner and saw a blue pickup truck pull up.

"Trevor's mother is the realtor that sold you that house." Mirabel turned toward her. "She sells everything in this town."

"I had no idea." Cassie glanced toward the front window of the diner. "I only saw Bonnie briefly when I first arrived, everything else has been done on the phone. She seems young to have a son Trevor's age."

"She is young." Mirabel poured herself a cup of coffee. "And she's raised her son on her own, mostly. She's had a boyfriend or two along the way, but none ever stuck."

"Why do you think that is?" Cassie looked back at Mirabel and noticed the way she flicked her eyes toward the ceiling.

"I don't like to speak ill of people." Mirabel looked away from the ceiling, back down at the surface of her coffee. "But Trevor did not make it easy on his mother. Too much like his father, I'd say."

"Who is his father?" Cassie's heart raced with the knowledge that she was digging into someone else's business, but she was too curious to not ask the question. If Trevor was a suspect, then she needed to know as much about him as she could.

"Was his father. At least, that's what most of us assume. He was a football star around here, but when he found out he was going to be a father, he took off. He'd drift back in now and then, but he was always lost in one addiction or another. It's been about ten years since he showed his face, so the general consensus is that he's probably not with us anymore." Mirabel sighed and rolled her coffee cup between her palms. "People give Trevor a hard time for being different, for being more focused on his art than he is on anything else, but I say he's a pretty good kid for what he's had to go through. Not everyone has it easy."

"That's for sure." Cassie's heart softened at the thought of the boy's chaotic upbringing. Her own father had been a steady force in her life until his passing. She couldn't imagine growing up without him. "Mirabel, can I ask you something?" She looked into her friend's eyes.

"Of course." Mirabel smiled, her expression open and eager.

"Who do you think killed Miles?" Cassie watched as Mirabel's smile faded, her brows knitted together, and her lips tightened. "You know so much about everyone around here, I'd just like to get your opinion."

"I'd rather not give it." Mirabel picked up her cup of coffee.

"I'm sorry, I didn't mean to upset you." Cassie's heart pounded as she detected the anger in Mirabel's voice.

"I know you're new around here, Cassie. I know that to you, these people are just strangers, far different than the people you are used to being around. But you're right, I do know a lot about everyone who lives here. I know a lot because I grew up here, because I've been serving them coffee and pie since I was a teenager. I've celebrated their victories, their birthdays, their anniversaries. I've grieved with them over their losses, I've fought for the sanctity of this town, at their sides. They're not just people to me, they're family. So, when you ask me, which member of my family do I think is a murderer, how do you think I should answer that?" Mirabel's eyes narrowed. "None of them. I hope it was none of them."

Silenced by Mirabel's passionate words, Cassie felt her heart sink. She hoped she hadn't damaged her friendship with Mirabel, but another concern also surfaced as she watched Mirabel walk away. If she hoped that it was no one in Little Leaf Creek that had murdered Miles, did that mean that some part of her hoped that it might have been Cassie?

CHAPTER 23

Cassie didn't have long to dwell on the possibility before Sebastian walked through the door of the diner and right up to the mug of coffee that Mirabel had left on the counter.

Sebastian glanced up at Cassie as he sat down at the counter.

"Good morning."

"Good morning, young man." Cassie smiled as she looked over his boyish features.

"Young?" Sebastian coughed and set his mug down. "It's been a while since anyone called me that."

"Really? I bet you still have to show ID for beer." Cassie tilted her head to the side and squinted at him. "You are old enough to drink, right?"

"Funny." Sebastian traced his thumb along the rim of his mug. "Just how old do you think I am?"

"Eh, maybe twenty-nine?" Cassie raised her eyebrows. "But you could pass for much younger."

"Twenty-nine." Sebastian gazed down at the surface of his coffee. "It's been a long time since I thought about being under thirty. Those were some interesting years."

"It couldn't have been that long." Cassie crossed her arms as she peered at him. There were a few creases in his forehead, the start of a few wrinkles around his lips, but that was from having the life of a farmer, wasn't it?

"I'll be thirty-seven in May." Sebastian met her eyes as his voice softened. "Maybe we could find a way to celebrate together?"

"Is that what you say to all the girls?" Cassie laughed to cover her shock. She'd never once considered that he could be so close to her age. Her own husband had been five years older, and perhaps she'd got used to being around an older crowd. "Did you want anything to go with that coffee?"

"A little more conversation will do." Sebastian met her eyes as he picked up the mug. "Rough night?"

"Why do you ask?" Cassie brushed a few loose strands of hair back from her eyes.

"It must have been rough if you spent it with Ollie." Sebastian smiled as he took a sip of his coffee.

"This town really has no secrets, huh?" Cassie shook her head as she smiled.

"I'm glad he was there." Sebastian set the mug down and looked straight into her eyes. "You need to be careful, Cassie."

Was that a threat? Uncertainty caused her spine to tingle as she stared back at him. "I'm trying to be."

"After being run off the road yesterday, and finding that note in your house, it might not be enough." Sebastian's eyes narrowed. "Maybe you should leave town for a bit."

"I don't think Oliver would be okay with that." Cassie shook her head. "Besides, if this is going to be my new home, I don't want to leave. I want to stick around and help figure all of this out."

"Isn't that what put you in danger in the first place?" Sebastian set the mug down. "What was so bad about your old life that you'd rather stay here, where someone wants to harm you?"

"There's nothing to go back to." Cassie's voice wavered as sorrow welled up within her. "I need to get back to work."

Cassie felt his eyes on her as she began to greet the customers that entered the diner. By the time she had a chance to look back at him, she found his seat at the counter empty.

By the end of the breakfast rush, she began to wonder why Sebastian had encouraged her to leave. Was he concerned that she might know too much? She'd gone from suspecting Tessa, to turning her suspicions on Sebastian. But there was one person who could have easily had access to her house, and who Oliver strongly suspected of being involved. Trevor. Having no idea who to trust, left her so uneasy that she had a hard time focusing on the customers. After getting a few orders mixed-up, Mirabel pulled her aside.

"Maybe you should take off for the day? It's getting quiet, and Sharon is on her way in."

"I'm sorry, Mirabel." Cassie tugged off her apron. "I've made a mess of things today."

"Don't worry about it, hon." Mirabel gave her shoulder a light pat. "We all have off days, and you've more than earned yours. I'll call you if it gets busy and I need you."

"You're right, I could use a break." Cassie hung up her apron, then headed for the door. It was time she had a very direct conversation with the one person she hoped wouldn't be guilty of murder.

~

As soon as Cassie left the diner, she dialed Trevor's number and waited for him to answer. It took three tries before he actually answered the phone.

"Why are you calling me?"

"Hello to you, too." Cassie did her best to sound cheerful. "Where are you? I'd love to discuss some things with you."

"I'm a little busy right now." Trevor cleared his throat. "Maybe later."

"Trevor, I really need to speak with you." Cassie listened to the sounds in the background of the call. "Are you in town?"

"I'm at the dump, okay?" Trevor ended the call.

Cassie stared at her phone for a moment and wondered whether she really wanted to go find him. If he was evading her calls, he might have a reason. Did he suspect her? Or did he suspect that she suspected him? There was only one way to find out. Just as she started toward her car, Rose and Charles stepped out of their car.

"Hello there, Cassie." Rose smiled at her. "So good to see you out and about. Charles and I were both worried when we heard that Ollie spent the night at your house." She glanced over at Charles and lowered her voice. "That never would have been proper in our day."

"I'm sure Oliver was just doing his duty." Charles patted Rose's arm.

"He was doing his best to keep me safe." Cassie heard her own words and felt them, too. Oliver really had gone out of his way to protect her, and she'd barely taken the time to thank him. "Maybe you could help me with something? I'm looking for the dump."

"The landfill?" Rose raised her eyebrows. "Why would you want to go there?"

"Just curious where it is, I guess." Cassie shrugged and slipped her cell phone into her purse. She didn't want to tell them that she was on her way to see Trevor. They might gossip about it. "Is it nearby?"

Charles pointed her in the right direction and added instructions on where to turn, then the pair headed into the diner.

Cassie hopped in her car, followed Charles' directions and soon found herself at the open gate of the town landfill. She spotted Trevor right away as he stood near the entrance. She noticed that he was wearing gloves.

"Trevor." Cassie paused a few feet away from him. "Can we talk?"

"I'm working." Trevor glanced over at her, then turned his attention back to the pile of items that he looked through.

"I can see that, and I don't mean to interrupt, but I was hoping we could talk for a minute." Cassie watched Trevor pick up a chunk of metal that might have once belonged to an appliance of some kind.

"Talk about what?" Trevor looked up at her, his eyes heavy. "Did you want to give me another pep talk about what I should charge? Or ask me what it's like to be thrust into the middle of a murder investigation? Do you know how close I was to being in handcuffs?"

"I'm sorry about that." Cassie shook her head as she squinted against the sun that glinted off the piece of metal he held. "I know all of this must be frightening for you."

"Frightening? No, it's more like expected. Anticipated." Trevor snatched a small sliver of metal from between two old couch cushions. "This town has been looking for a reason to hate me since I was born. It's my fault their hero turned into a nightmare." He smiled as he looked up at her. "Or haven't you heard the grand tale of my birth?"

"I have." Cassie studied him. "But what your father did, has nothing to do with you."

"Wrong, according to this town, it has everything to do with me." Trevor sighed as he stared back at her. "Why would you ever want to move here? Why would you want to subject yourself to this kind of nonsense?"

"I needed a change. I grew up in a small town like this. It wasn't always perfect, but it had something that my life in the city didn't. A sense of community." Cassie smiled. "I guess I am hoping to find that here."

"And how is that going for you?" Trevor laughed. "Do you feel welcomed in? Part of the family?"

"I think there are a lot of good people here." Cassie sensed the tension in his voice. Trevor wasn't just an outcast, he was also an outsider. He felt as if the town had turned against him. Did that make him a killer? "I'd love the chance to get to know them. But it's going to take time."

"You might be right about that, but as far as I'm concerned, I'm out of time. I've given these people my whole life, and they're all ready to lock me up and throw away the key. They all think I'm a murderer." Trevor smiled some. "I guess you should be happy about that."

"Why would you think that, Trevor?" Cassie's eyes widened.

"Because it's either you or me, isn't it?" Trevor squinted at her. "The outsider or the outlaw? Which one is it going to be?"

"Trevor, I just want to know if you spoke to Miles that day, before he was killed. If you did see him, if you argued with him, tell me." Cassie took a step closer to him. "I want to try to help you, but if you don't tell me the truth, I can't do that."

"Sure, you want me to confess that I had it out with Miles, so that you can run back to good old Ollie and tell him that Trevor is the murderer he suspects he is, and you can have your good life, your second chance at a community, while I rot in prison." Trevor stared straight into her eyes. "Sorry lady, no amount of overpaying me for my art is going to earn you a get out of jail free card from me. I'm not going to be locked up, there's no chance. I'll disappear before Ollie can get his hands on me."

"Trevor, I don't know what I can do to make you believe me, but I'm not trying to cause you any harm here." Cassie frowned as she scrutinized his hardened expression. "I believe in you, and your art.

But running away isn't going to get you anywhere. Do you really think Oliver is going to let you slip away?"

"I'm not going to give him another option. I'm just waiting for my paycheck, then I'm out of here." Trevor stepped closer to her. "And if I were you, I'd do the same thing."

"What about your mother?" Cassie took a step toward him. "You don't want to leave her behind, do you?"

"My mother?" Trevor laughed, then looked up at the sky. "The best thing I can do for her is to leave her behind. She's been apologizing for me her whole life. She could use the break." He looked back at her. "Whether or not I saw Miles, doesn't matter. What matters is why he's dead. I had no reason to kill him. It's not like my art hasn't been rejected millions of times." He shook his head. "Someone wanted him dead, but they wanted to make it look like it was me, or maybe even you." He shrugged. "One of us is going to go down, and while I think it's great that you love my art, I'm not going to go to prison for you, Cassie."

"Do you really think I killed Miles?" Cassie stared into his eyes. "Does it seem like I'm capable of something like that?"

"No more than me." Trevor's lips drew into a thin, tight line, then he sighed. "But like I said, it doesn't matter. One of us is going down for this, it's only a matter of time. But I'm not going to be here to take the fall." He turned and strode away.

Cassie stepped back out through the gate of the landfill and tried to hold back her frustration. She still didn't think that Trevor had killed Miles, but she wasn't any closer to proving who did.

CHAPTER 24

*A*s Cassie parked in her driveway, she caught sight of Tessa on her porch. She stepped out as Tessa waved her over.

"Let's talk."

Tessa's words sounded like an invitation, but her tone sounded more like a command. She stared at her for a moment, as she wondered whether she wanted to talk with her in her house. Maybe, she would find something inside that would tell her for sure that it was Tessa that had threatened her. She closed her car door, and crossed the distance between their two houses. She paused at Tessa's door and met her eyes.

"Come on now, or you're going to let the dog out." Tessa frowned.

Cassie crossed the threshold with her breath caught in her throat. Was this a foolish move?

"I sent a text to Mirabel to let her know I'd be here, in case she can't reach me, and needs to find me." Cassie stumbled over her words, with each one spoken feeling more and more awkward. She felt foolish fearing being alone with the older woman, but Tessa was strong, and with her experience in the police force she was sure she had the knowledge and skills to kill Miles.

"Oh?" Tessa led her into the kitchen. "Did you tell her that you were visiting Trevor, too?"

"How did you know about that?" Cassie's eyes widened.

"I saw you two talking to each other at the landfill when I drove past." Tessa set out two plates on the counter. "There's still plenty of cake to eat."

"I just wanted to talk with him about what happened. I thought maybe if I could look him in the eyes, maybe he would tell me the truth about whether he met up with Miles that day." Cassie bent down to stroke Harry's ears, then sank down in one of the kitchen chairs as Tessa cut them each a slice of cake.

"So, what do you think? Did he meet with Miles?"

Tessa placed a slice of cake on a plate, then set it down on the table in front of Cassie.

Cassie gazed at the homemade frosting that hugged the corner of the slice and felt her mouth water. It looked delicious and from tasting it before she knew it tasted as good as it looked.

"I don't know." Cassie picked up her fork.

"You don't know?" Tessa sat down across from her with her own slice of cake. "You just spoke with him, you asked him questions, how do you not know? What do your instincts tell you?"

"I don't know." Cassie continued to stare at the cake.

"Cassie, that's not true. Your instincts are telling you something, you just don't want to admit it." Tessa stared straight at Cassie as she looked up at her. "You're going to have to admit it sooner or later, you might as well tell me the truth."

"I don't know what the truth is, Tessa." Cassie's eyes narrowed as she stared back at her. "I have no idea who to believe, who to trust. All I know is that I didn't kill Miles, and yet me arriving here set all of this into motion. I thought I was making the right choice."

"Don't do that." Tessa shook her head as she dug her fork into her slice of cake.

"Don't do what?"

"Don't ignore your instincts." Tessa looked up at Cassie and met her eyes. "You say you're innocent, then you need to prove it, and the one way you prove it is by figuring out who is guilty."

"But I don't know who did it?" Cassie sank down in her chair.

"You'll have to figure it out." Tessa set down her fork, then wiped her mouth with a napkin. "I know you've been through a lot with losing your husband but you need to look toward the future. Once the real murderer is found, you can move forward."

"I hope so." Cassie's chest tightened at the mention of her husband. News about her past was obviously spreading around town.

"Cassie, stop worrying so much and eat some cake." Tessa chuckled as she picked up her fork again. "Everything will fall into place."

Cassie dug into the moist cake. As she looked up at Tessa again, she noticed a faint gleam in her eyes.

"I'm never sure how to take you, Tessa. You've been so kind to me, but at the same time, it seems like you'd rather be alone." Cassie took a bite of the cake. "I'm still not sure why you're helping me."

"No? You haven't figured it out, yet?" Tessa quirked an eyebrow as she gazed at her. "Maybe, if we figure out who actually killed Miles, you can stop looking at me like I might be a murderer, like I might just be out to get you."

The cake melted on Cassie's tongue, the sweet frosting made the taste even smoother, but the way Tessa looked at her made her feel as if she'd just swallowed something sour. Had she been able to read her so well the entire time? That seemed impossible to her.

"I don't think you're out to get me." Cassie swallowed the remainder of the cake in her mouth, but it felt as if it stuck in her throat.

"Do anything you want, Cassie, I'm not one to tell anyone what to do. But I'm asking you, please, tell me the truth." Tessa frowned. "It's okay to suspect me. It's okay to think I might just be the type that could murder someone. Just don't pretend that you're not thinking it."

"Why did you leave Little Leaf Creek?" Cassie narrowed her eyes, determined to change the subject.

"No reason." Tessa cleared her throat. "Just needed a change."

Cassie could tell there was more to the story but she didn't think Tessa would tell her more about it, at least not yet.

"You told me that you taught Oliver everything he knows." Cassie tried to catch her eye. "But now the two of you barely talk. What's that about?"

"That's something between him and me." Tessa shrugged and took another bite of her cake.

"He's a detective, and he has a problem with you, which makes me think that you might have a problem with the law." Cassie raised her eyebrows. "You say you want to be my friend, but you don't want to tell me anything real?"

"Okay." Tessa set her fork down and looked up at her. "Do you want to hear something real?" She smiled.

"Yes, I do." Cassie watched her as her heart pounded.

"Oliver could have been a great detective, but instead he's settled for being stuck here in Little Leaf Creek, investigating pie theft and shoplifting." Tessa shrugged. "We don't see eye to eye when it comes to certain things."

"Pie theft, really?" Cassie smiled as she took another bite of her cake.

"Don't laugh, Mrs. Right down the street is still recovering from the blueberry pie incident this past spring." Tessa pointed her finger at Cassie. "It's nothing to smile about."

"Is this your way of avoiding the question?" Cassie shook her head.

"Maybe it's my way of showing you that you can relax around me, even though you still suspect I might be a murderer." Tessa picked up her empty plate, stacked it on top of Cassie's and set it in the sink. "Now, about Trevor."

"Yes, about Trevor." Oliver's voice drifted into the kitchen from the front of the house.

CHAPTER 25

"Oliver?" Tessa walked toward the door. "What are you doing here?"

"I need to speak to Cassie." Oliver crossed the living room and paused in the entrance of the kitchen. "Did you go to see Trevor?"

"Yes." Cassie stood up from her chair. "Why?"

"I need to know where he is." Oliver stepped closer to her. "Where was he when you last saw him?"

"At the landfill." Cassie frowned as she crossed her arms. "What is this all about?"

"I confirmed Sebastian's alibi for the time of the murder. I have three witnesses that place him in the hardware store, and nowhere near your house when

Miles was killed. I also have proof that Trevor and Miles met that day, only minutes before Miles' body was found. I have a witness that attests that they were arguing." Oliver looked into her eyes. "Did he say where he was going?"

"No, he didn't." Cassie's mind raced to catch up with what he said. "I don't understand what is going on here, just because he had an argument with Miles, that doesn't mean that he's the killer."

"It all adds up, Cassie. He had motive, he was nearby, and he could have easily had full access to your house to leave that threatening note. Now, he has disappeared, indicating he's feeling pretty guilty about something." Oliver held her gaze. "I need you to tell me everything he said to you when you spoke to him."

"Or maybe you just suspect him because he's an easy target!" Cassie's heart slammed against her chest. "He's just a kid who never stood a chance in this town!"

"Cassie, I need to know where he is." Oliver's tone remained calm. "Speaking to him will help me figure out if he's guilty or not, but I can't do that if you don't tell me where he is. I am trying to narrow down my suspects, that's all. Trevor is one of them, and I need to see him again to clear him."

"Your suspects?" Cassie crossed her arms. "Aren't I on that list? I had just as much motive, and just as much opportunity as Trevor."

"I'm not here for you, I'm here for Trevor." Oliver paused, then took a breath. "But I'll probably be back for you, and for Tessa." He turned his attention to the silent woman. "I don't have a bias when it comes to an investigation, whether you're an enemy, a friend, or a stranger, you get treated equally by me."

"Trevor has never been in my house." Cassie shook her head.

"But he could have got the key." Oliver looked at Cassie. "Did you check the envelope when you got it?"

"No, I never checked that there were three keys in there." Cassie shook her head. "Maybe there never was a third key."

"Really anyone could have broken in." Oliver looked at Tessa.

"You suspect me?" Tessa pointed at herself, her eyes narrowed. "Do you really think I could steal, murder someone, and then threaten Cassie? Do you really think I could have done this, Cassie?"

"No, I don't know what to think." Cassie held out her hands and shook her head. "I don't know who broke in without leaving a trace. I don't know who could have taken the key."

"Someone did it, someone took the key. Sebastian has an alibi for the time of the murder." Oliver glanced at Tessa again.

"Really? Do you think I just decided to go out and murder Miles because he looked at me funny once a dozen years ago?" Tessa shook her head.

"There was a lot more than just that between the two of you. You never got along." Oliver's even tone didn't hint at any emotion he might be feeling.

"That was years ago, simple." Tessa shook her head.

"It's not that simple. I have to investigate everyone. You and Miles never got along. Then when he managed to stop your plans to build a big barn for your goats where you wanted it, you were furious with him. You never forgave him for making you build a smaller barn on the other side of your property. You refused to even speak to him after that." Oliver straightened his shoulders. "You don't have an alibi for the time of the murder."

"I don't, but I also didn't enter Cassie's house before it was broken into." Tessa glanced at Cassie.

"You could have broken in easily. Maybe there wasn't a third key or maybe you took the key to divert the suspicion from yourself and to ensure that you had easy access to the house in the future." Oliver narrowed his eyes.

"That's quite a story. Look, it's very simple, son." Tessa walked toward him. "You either put those cuffs on me right now, or you need to get out of my house."

"Tessa!" Oliver's voice wavered as he stared at her. "Don't do this. You know I have to investigate everyone."

"Don't do what?" Tessa raised her eyebrows. "Demand my rights? You two are both in my house, and I've asked you both to leave, now. If you don't have enough evidence to arrest me, which I know that you don't, then you need to turn around and leave please."

"Tessa, you know I have people I have to answer to." Oliver sharpened his tone.

"Yes, and I'm one of them." Tessa shot a brief look in Cassie's direction. "Cassie, I can understand. She doesn't know me. I don't like it, after everything I've done for her, but I can understand it." She looked at Oliver. "But you? You know me."

"I have to do my job." Oliver took a step back, then looked over at Cassie. "It's time for us to leave."

Cassie couldn't bring herself to speak. She felt as

if she had betrayed Tessa by not defending her, but how could she, she didn't know her. She didn't think she was a murderer, but what could she base that on.

"Go on." Tessa followed them toward the door. "Just keep in mind, Oliver, I taught you better than this."

Oliver looked back at her, his dark eyes heavy with emotion as they locked to Tessa's. "I'm going to find out who killed Miles, and whoever it is, is getting locked up for good. That's what you taught me to do, Tessa."

As the door slammed closed behind her, Cassie jumped.

"It's alright, don't take it personally. She only slams the door on people she likes." Oliver offered a strained smile.

"There's nothing funny about any of this." Cassie groaned as she descended the steps of Tessa's front porch. "You should have just believed me when I said that I don't know where Trevor is."

"How can I?" Oliver followed after her. "You've made it clear that you think he's innocent, and you will do what it takes to protect him."

"Because I think he is innocent." Cassie turned around to face him, her voice strained by the pounding of her heart. "You've wasted all this time focusing on an innocent man, and an innocent woman, while a killer roams free on the streets of your town!"

"Our town." Oliver looked into her eyes. "Cassie, I'm not letting anyone roam free. I'm close, I can feel it."

"Then go do your job." Cassie shook her head as she turned around and walked back toward her house. "Come back and tell me when you have the actual murderer in custody." She glanced back at Tessa's house and felt her heart sink. She'd been a good friend to her, and she hadn't defended her when Oliver practically accused her of murder. Maybe the move to Little Leaf Creek wasn't the right choice. Maybe there was no way to get the community and friendships that she'd hoped for, because she was the one that didn't belong.

Cassie closed her door behind her and turned the lock. As she recalled that she'd yet to pick up the new locks from the hardware store, she walked over to the couch and sat on it. She could put her house back on the market. She could move on to another town. She could try it all over again and leave this chaos behind. But as she closed her eyes, she felt that connection she'd been seeking despite what had happened there. She couldn't walk away. Little Leaf Creek had become her home in the few short days she'd been there. She couldn't leave it, not while a murderer was on the loose, and its residents were at each other's throats.

CHAPTER 26

Cassie closed her eyes and imagined Miles walking up to her front lawn. He saw the statue. Maybe he formed an opinion about it. Maybe he argued with Trevor over the worth of his art. The anger between them was loud enough to draw the attention of a few witnesses. But Trevor walked away.

Didn't he? She squeezed her eyes shut tighter and tried to picture Miles' next moments. Who did he see? Who did he talk to? If he'd had the chance to tell anyone where he was going, who would it have been?

Cassie's eyes snapped open. The historical society. He would have checked in with them on his way to the statue. If anyone knew more about his final moments, it had to be them. Rose and Charles had mentioned that he contacted them on the way to the statue, but they didn't mention if he said he was meeting with anyone else. She didn't want to speak to them about it and risk antagonizing them again, but there were other members of the historical society who might be able to help. She pulled out her phone and dialed Mirabel's number.

"Cassie, do you miss me already?" Mirabel laughed into the phone. "The diner can survive without you, I promise."

"Mirabel, do you know how I can get in contact with Avery and Karen from the historical society?" Breathless, Cassie grabbed her purse and her keys, then hurried out the door.

"You can come have lunch with them if you'd like. They're here. Is everything okay?"

"Yes, I'll be there soon." Cassie ended the call as she reached her car. Just when she pulled the door open, she noticed Tessa on her front porch. She stared out at her as she started her car.

Tessa's heavy gaze left her unsettled. Was she plotting revenge? Did she decide that she needed to get rid of her, too?

Cassie pushed the thought from her mind as she

drove to the diner. Moments later she stepped inside.

"Cassie!" Avery waved to her. "Mirabel said you wanted to speak with us." She nodded to Karen. "We're just enjoying a late lunch after a busy morning, you're welcome to join us."

"Thank you so much." Cassie sat down at their table. "What were you up to this morning?"

"We had a terrible meeting." Karen rolled her eyes. "That awful man who is trying to open the sports bar in town just threw a complete tantrum."

"A tantrum?" Cassie looked between them. "What do you mean?"

"Apparently he felt he had some kind of arrangement with Miles, an agreement that he could redo the outside of the bar to make it look more modern and add in loud music and television screens." Avery scrunched up her nose. "As if we'd ever let that happen."

"It's not like Miles would have asked us." Karen flicked her hair back over her shoulder. "We're learning that he had quite a few arrangements going on."

"Any that went sour like this one?" Cassie pulled out her notepad to take notes.

"It's going to take some untangling to figure all of

that out. But you should have seen Rose and Charles, they were absolutely livid. I think if Miles had still been alive, they would have been at his throat." Avery sighed. "This group was set up for the sake of our town, but it looks like Miles was taking advantage of his position. You see, the historical society doesn't make the final choice about a project, the town council does that, but it takes our opinion very highly. Miles had been getting his palms greased and going straight to the town council with his approval, without the rest of us even knowing. The council had assumed he represented the entire, or at least the majority, of the historical society's opinion." She shook her head. "It's tough to lose a friend and then find out he wasn't the person you thought he was in the first place."

"It's like losing someone twice." Karen lowered her voice. "It's been rough on all of us. And that man certainly didn't make it any easier with his rantings."

"Are you sure that Miles did this voluntarily?" Cassie looked from Karen to Avery. "What if he wasn't given a choice? What if someone was threatening him?"

"It sure doesn't seem that way." Avery scrunched up her nose. "It all makes sense now. He always had so much money to throw around, even though he didn't have a very well-paying job and he retired early."

"If Miles was taking bribes, then maybe he didn't follow through on one of them. If that was the case, then whoever paid him might have been angry enough to kill him." Cassie sighed as she wiped a hand across her face. "Which brings me to the reason that I'm here. Did Miles contact any of you about meeting with Trevor before he went to my house?"

"Not either of us." Avery shook her head. "But he didn't talk to us as much as he talked to Rose and Charles. They're the original three members of the historical society, others have moved on or passed away, and we're their replacements."

"They consider us junior members." Karen snorted. "Of course, we're expected to do twice as much work."

"Did Rose and Charles mention anything about him meeting with Trevor?" Cassie looked between the two of them as she sensed some tension form in the looks they exchanged.

"We know that Miles went to speak to Fred, the owner of the sports bar. Then he planned on checking out your statue. That's all we know, and we've told the police that, too." Karen frowned as she looked at Cassie. "Maybe you should just let this go. Snooping around is no way to make a good impression in a new town."

"Maybe you're right. Thanks for your time." Cassie stood up from the table and headed for the door. As she walked through it, Mirabel chased after her.

"Cassie! You still didn't collect your tip from the other day!" Mirabel waved her hand as Cassie approached her car.

"I'll get it later, thanks Mirabel." Cassie didn't want to spare a second. She needed to talk to Fred again. If he saw Miles just before he died, he might know what was on his mind and had a clue to who killed him. Cassie parked in front of Fred's bar and tried the front door. It swung open, despite the building being dark.

"Fred? Are you here?" Cassie poked her head inside and felt a rush of apprehension. Fred had said that he was relying on Miles to sway the council to approve of his renovations. What if Miles had changed his mind? What if he had decided to demand a larger bribe from Fred, knowing that Fred had already invested in the renovations?

"I'm here." Fred stepped out through a door behind the bar. "Cassie, what are you doing here?"

"Just popped in for a chat." Cassie walked toward him as she felt his eyes on her. Something was different about him, about the way he looked at her. When she drew closer to him, she identified exactly what it was. Fred reeked of alcohol. "Are you doing okay?"

"Am I doing okay?" Fred offered a lopsided smile. "I invested everything I had in this place, on the guarantee that my old high school buddy gave me, that he would take care of the red tape. But he didn't."

"He couldn't." Cassie frowned as she met his eyes. "Did you talk to him that day, Fred? Did you two argue?"

"I wanted to know what the holdup was with the paperwork, everything was supposed to be approved. He came to the bar to sweet talk me." Fred sneered, then shook his head. "I finally got out of him that the other members of the historical society were fighting him on the approval. It wasn't as easy as he claimed it would be when he took my money." He narrowed his eyes.

"That must have made you pretty angry." Cassie studied his expression as it grew more tense.

"Of course, it did. He'd assured me of things that he didn't follow through on. I was going to tell him exactly what I thought of him, but he got a call that he had to take, and he was gone." Fred shook his head. "I never should have let him walk out that door. Maybe if I hadn't, he'd still be alive, and I wouldn't be facing bankruptcy."

"You said he got a call? Do you know who it was from?" Cassie rested her phone on the bar between them, her eyes focused on his.

"He called the person on the phone Tessa. He said something like, you need to calm down, Tessa. I presume it must have been Tessa Watters." Fred shook his head as he sighed. "I already told all of this to Detective Graham."

"You told the detective that Miles was on the phone with Tessa right before he was killed?" Cassie's eyes widened.

"Yes, I did. Not that it seemed to make any difference." Fred slapped his hand against the top of the bar. "I'm sorry, I don't want to talk about this anymore. I've got to figure out how I'm going to save my business, before it's too late." He met her eyes again. "I don't know how you've got yourself so wrapped up in this, but take it from me, Cassie, the people around here can't be trusted."

Cassie felt the weight of his words, as she left the bar and drove back to her house.

CHAPTER 27

*C*assie settled her gaze on Tessa's house as she walked toward her front door. She thought at first that she might be someone that she could trust, but in all the time they had spent discussing Miles' murder, never once had she mentioned that she spoke to Miles on the phone.

Cassie didn't know exactly what happened between Miles and Tessa, but she knew it was enough for Fred to mention it. And maybe, just maybe, Oliver's history with Tessa was enough reason for him to want to cover up Tessa's involvement. It made her feel terrible to think that she'd been played by them from the very start. When she started digging, did Tessa decide it was time to warn her to stop?

Cassie had just closed her door when she heard a light knock on it. She pulled it open and saw two warm smiles on two familiar faces.

"Rose, Charles." She smiled at them both. "I was just talking about you."

"You were?" Rose's smile spread wider. She grasped a picnic basket in one hand. "What a fun coincidence. We're here to kidnap you."

"What?" Cassie stared at them both as she laughed.

"Rose, don't be so dramatic." Charles rolled his eyes.

"We just feel like you've had such a hard go of it here." Rose switched the picnic basket from one hand to the other and smiled at her. "We want to show you just how beautiful this town can be."

"That's very kind of you." Cassie felt some relief as she looked between the two. "But I wouldn't want to take up any of your time. I'm really okay."

"Nonsense." Charles frowned as he wrapped his arm around hers. "How can you be? You've been through so much, and with the way Detective Graham behaved, inviting himself to stay in your home overnight, I can only imagine that you want to get out of here as soon as possible. I do hope that a little tour of the most beautiful places Little Leaf

Creek has to offer will change your mind about that." He guided her down the porch steps. "Just come with us for a couple of hours, and I'm sure we'll have you cheered up."

"That sounds lovely." Cassie smiled as she looked into his eyes. This was the sense of community that she had been looking for, someone to make her feel as if she belonged, and that they cared about what happened to her. She decided to allow them to take her on their tour. Maybe some time in nature would provide her the clarity she needed to figure out just how Tessa had pulled off the murder.

As Cassie settled in the back seat of Charles' car, she reviewed the moments after the murder in her mind. When she'd first seen Tessa after finding Miles, she'd noticed something, something that hadn't stuck out in her mind until now. Her clean white t-shirt. Had she run inside to change?

A bump in the road jolted Cassie out of her thoughts as Charles pulled into an area of the woods.

"We'll walk from here." Charles turned the car off.

Cassie stepped out of the car and took a deep breath of the fresh air. Already she felt better, and closer to the heart of Little Leaf Creek than she had since she arrived.

"Gorgeous, isn't it?" Rose raked her gaze along the long branches full of lush, dark green leaves. "Wait until you see it in the fall." She looped her arm around Cassie's and led her along a narrow path through the trees.

Cassie walked for some time, drinking in the natural scenery around her. The tweeting birds and chattering squirrels soothed her nerves to the point that she wondered why she was caught up trying to help solve the murder.

"This is a good spot." Charles set the picnic basket down on the ground near a large, flat rock. "We even have our own table."

"It's great." Cassie took another deep breath of the crisp air and smiled at both of them. "I can't thank you enough. If it weren't for you, I would probably be at home moping about my luck. Thanks to you both, I feel a lot better."

"That's good, dear." Rose smiled at her, then looked over at Charles. "See, didn't I tell you it was a good idea?"

"Yes, you did, darling." Charles walked over to her and wrapped his arm around her shoulders. "I'm so glad we were able to get away together, just the three of us. It's been so long since we've been out here. Not many people know about the trail that leads out to this spot. It's not on any maps."

"I'm so grateful you decided to share it with me." Cassie sat down on the edge of the rock and looked out through the multitude of trees that surrounded them. "It's like being in a whole different world."

"It is, isn't it." Charles stepped away from Rose and walked toward Cassie. "I know that you came here because you wanted a different kind of life, Cassie." He paused in front of her. "Because of that, I think you'll understand why Rose and I had to do what we did."

"What do you mean?" Cassie looked up at him as he placed his hands on her shoulders.

"You've lived a different way for so long. In a large city in which there's no sense of community spirit, there's no sense of neighborly support. So, when you suffered such a tragedy, you decided to leave. The saddest part about that is that so many places are becoming just like that. We're running out of quiet places, where history is still an important part of everyday life. Without these small safe harbors we can't begin to imagine what our future might be like. I don't even want to picture it." Charles' voice trembled as he looked over at Rose. "We've invested many years of our lives in this town, in this world, and the thought of spending our final years watching it all fall apart, or be ripped apart by greed and modernization, it's just not something that we can tolerate."

"It's inspiring to find someone as passionate as you two are about preserving places like this." Cassie placed her hands over his and searched his eyes. "I'm sure everyone in Little Leaf Creek is very grateful for all of the hard work you've done."

"For the things they know about." Rose stepped up beside her husband. "But there are things that they can never know about. I hope you understand, it's just bad luck that you ended up here."

"I think it's pretty good luck, actually." Cassie laughed as she looked between them. "I've had the chance to meet you two, how could that be bad?"

"I'm so sorry, Cassie, really I am." Charles shifted his hands suddenly. He pressed his palms against the sides of her neck and wrapped his fingers around it.

"What are you doing?" Cassie gasped as she pulled at his hands. "You're hurting me!"

"Don't bother to scream, dear, it won't do you any good." Rose ran her hand down through Cassie's hair in a soothing motion. "It's what's best for Little Leaf Creek, we all must make sacrifices."

CHAPTER 28

Cassie clawed at Charles' hands and struggled against his grasp. As her thoughts blurred between panic and shock, she began to put two and two together. The high heel marks that Oliver had found near her back door, must have been made by Rose. Tessa mentioned their son was a mechanic in town. Is that where they got Sebastian's blue pickup truck?

"You ran me off the road! It was you who left that note!" Cassie gasped out as she tried to shove Charles' hands away. "You used Sebastian's car! You broke into my house!"

"Like a common criminal?" Rose laughed and shook her head. "We didn't need to break in, sweetheart. We make it our business to try and get a key to all the historical homes in the area. You may own the house, but it really belongs to Little Leaf Creek, that's something that will never change. When you left your purse on your chair at the table at the diner, I managed to get the spare key. I know the envelope Bonnie uses for the spare keys, so it was easy to spot. It came in so handy." She frowned as she gazed at Cassie. "I had really hoped we could be friends, Cassie, but you just don't love Little Leaf Creek the way we do."

Cassie gasped and tugged at Charles' hands, but his grip only got tighter. Her mind spun, as darkness crept in at the edges of her vision. She knew in minutes, or maybe even seconds, everything would be over. With a final burst of strength, she slammed her knee up against Charles' stomach. The blow barely struck him, but it was enough to surprise him. She felt his grasp release some and used the moment to lunge away from him. With each stride she took she expected his hands to be back around her neck again. She didn't dare to look back at him as she ran for the trees.

"Get her, Charles!" Rose shrieked. "You can't let her get away!"

Cassie heard Charles' footsteps pounding against the ground behind her. She knew he was only a few steps away and pushed herself to run faster. As her legs and lungs began to burn, she risked a glance back over her shoulder to see where he was. To her surprise, he was no longer behind her. She slowed a little, then turned back in an attempt to find the trail. The moment she did, she slammed into Sebastian's chest.

"Sebastian!" Cassie gasped as she looked into his eyes. "Help me please!"

"Cassie! Thank goodness I found you!" Sebastian wrapped his arms around her.

"It was Rose and Charles! They're the ones who killed Miles, and they're trying to kill me, too!" Cassie glanced over her shoulder again. "Charles was chasing me, I don't know where he is, now!"

"Okay, stay close to me." Sebastian tangled his fingers with hers and gripped her hand tight as he peered through the trees. "They could be anywhere."

"You believe me?" Cassie squeezed his hand.

"Of course, I do." Sebastian looked over at her for a long moment, then turned his attention back to the trees. "We need to get you to safety. We need to get back on the trail."

"No, we can't, he'll find me." Cassie shuddered at the memory of his hands around her neck.

"It's okay, Cassie, I'm not the only one coming to

your rescue. We're not alone out here." Sebastian nodded to a few officers who had begun moving through the trees.

Startled, Cassie clung tighter to Sebastian's hand. She'd never been so happy to see anyone in her life. "Okay, but they're clever, and they know these woods."

"I know." Sebastian guided her to the edge of the trail, where more officers were moving up it, back to the clearing that Charles found. "I'll take you down to the road." He started to steer her in that direction.

"No." Cassie took a deep breath. "I know where they were, I can lead the officers to them." She started up the path.

"Cassie, aren't you scared?" Sebastian tugged her back toward him.

"Not as scared as I'll be if they aren't caught." Cassie forced one foot in front of the other until she could see the clearing with the large, flat rock. There was the overturned picnic basket, and not far from it was Rose. She peered into the woods on the other side of the clearing.

"Charles! Charles, did you find her?" Rose took a step back as Charles emerged from the tree line.

"Not yet, but I will." Charles snarled his words. "I

knew we should have just killed her at her house, just like we should have killed Miles at the overlook when we had the chance, this whole idea was too much."

"Oh? And how did you think you'd keep Tessa from hearing her screams? You know she made it clear that she was looking out for Cassie. Between Tessa's nosiness, her dog and her goats, someone would have been alerted and we would have been found out." Rose slapped her hands together. "Go get her! This is not the time to argue!"

"Hands in the air!"

Cassie recognized the voice immediately. It belonged to Oliver. He stepped out of the woods behind Charles, with his gun aimed at his back. "Make a move and I will pull the trigger! Don't test me!"

"Ollie!" Rose huffed. "Ollie, you need to just stay out of this! What would your father think of you pointing a gun at his old friend?"

"He'd think I'd better cuff you both for the murder of another of his old friends, and the attempted murder of an innocent woman." Oliver continued to point his gun at Charles as several other officers stepped forward.

Cassie looked away, but she could hear the

sounds of the arrests taking place. The click of the cuffs, the monotonous reciting of their rights.

"It's okay now." Sebastian pulled her close and kissed the top of her head. "You're safe now."

"How did you even know I was out here?" Cassie stared into his eyes, still stunned by the entire event, but even more surprised that he had shown up just when she needed him to.

"I was asking around for you." Sebastian frowned as he shook his head. "I'd stopped in at the diner, and Mirabel said that she hadn't seen you. She gave me this note and tip to take to you that Rose had left behind for you." He pulled the note from his pocket. Cassie skimmed over the note. It was an apology from Rose on behalf of Charles because of the way he acted toward Cassie at the diner, suspecting her of the murder. "When I saw the handwriting, I knew it was the same as the threatening note that you found on your countertop. Then I knew it had to be Rose and Charles that were threatening you and killed Miles." He looked over at the pair. "It was hard for me to believe, but I needed to find you to warn you. So, I went to your house and saw the three of you just as you pulled away. I tried to follow you, but Charles lost me along the way. That's when I called Oliver."

Sebastian nodded toward the police officers that surrounded them.

"I told him everything I suspected, and that Rose and Charles might be trying to hurt you. So, he initiated a manhunt. But it was really Tessa that saved you." He pulled his phone out of his pocket. "I called her after I called Oliver and asked her if she knew any place that Rose and Charles might take you. She said that there was a trail not on any of the maps that very few people know about. I followed her directions and was able to find it. When I saw Rose and Charles' car, I knew you had to be here."

"I didn't think I was ever going to make it out of these woods, Sebastian. Without you, without all of you, I wouldn't be alive right now."

"I'm sorry I didn't get to you sooner."

"I'm just so glad you were here to help me." Cassie gazed into his eyes.

"Always." Sebastian winked.

"The ambulance can't get up here, it'll be quicker if we take her down to them ourselves." Oliver reached his hand out to her as he stood over Sebastian. "Let's go, you need to get checked out."

"I'm fine." Cassie looked up at him, reluctant to leave the warmth of Sebastian's arm around her.

"You don't know that, Cassie. There's a lot of

bruising and swelling. There could have been damage done that you don't know about, yet." Oliver met her eyes. "Please, I'll make sure you get there safe."

"He's right." Sebastian pulled his arm away. "It's best to make sure that you're okay."

Cassie took Oliver's hand and held it. She noticed fear in his eyes as he looked at her.

"I'm sorry, Cassie, I should have figured out that it was Rose and Charles, then you never would have been in danger." Oliver led her toward the trail out to the small parking area.

"It's not your fault, Oliver." Cassie squeezed his hand. "No one would have suspected the two of them. They seemed sweet and kind. At least most of the time."

"Maybe if I hadn't been distracted," Oliver muttered, as he pushed away some thin branches to clear the way for her.

"You had a lot on your plate." Cassie frowned. "You did everything you could, I know that."

"That wasn't what distracted me." Oliver cleared his throat as he reached the end of the trail.

"What do you mean?" Cassie met his eyes.

"After all of this it might be best if you leave Little Leaf Creek, Cassie." Oliver's shoulders tensed as he studied her. "No one would blame you if you did."

"If I had still been living in the city, and someone tried to hunt me down, they would have gotten to me." Cassie held his gaze. "No one would have come to look for me, no one would have thought twice about it. But because of this community, because of its kindness, I was saved. It may take some time for the rest of the town to accept me, but Little Leaf Creek is my home, now. I'm not going anywhere."

"Great." Oliver tilted his head toward the waiting ambulance. "Go get checked out, then I'll need to take your statement. We have a lot to sort through."

As Cassie walked over to the ambulance, she glanced back and caught him watching her. She couldn't tell if he was pleased she'd decided to stay, or annoyed. As the medics began to look her over, another familiar face appeared around the door of the ambulance.

"You're still breathing?" Tessa grinned.

"Thanks to you." Cassie swallowed back a rush of guilt. "Tessa, I'm so sorry."

"You have nothing to apologize for." Tessa leaned into the ambulance and put her hand on Cassie's shoulder.

"Of course, I do. I really thought you were

involved." Cassie winced. "Especially, once I found out you'd spoken to Miles before he was killed, and never told me about it."

"I'm sorry about that, Cassie, I shouldn't have kept it from you. I thought I could convince him to take it easy on your statue. I had hoped that he would be reasonable about it, and when he wasn't, I might have lost my temper a little. It's not the kind of thing I wanted to get out during a murder investigation. So, I thought it best to keep it to myself."

"You went to bat for me?" Cassie smiled as she met her eyes. "You really do like me don't you, Tessa?"

"You're one of the few, kid." Tessa winked at her, then her smile faded. "Little towns have their secrets, Cassie, and soon enough you'll discover them. I just hope that we can share a slice of cake while we figure them out."

"That sounds delicious." Cassie sighed as she recalled the taste of Tessa's cake. Yes, Little Leaf Creek definitely had its secrets, but so did she, she would fit in just fine.

The End

ABOUT THE AUTHOR

Cindy Bell is a USA Today and Wall Street Journal Bestselling Author. She is the author of the Little Leaf Creek, Wagging Tail, Donut Truck, Dune House, Sage Gardens, Chocolate Centered, Macaron Patisserie, Nuts about Nuts, Bekki the Beautician, Heavenly Highland Inn and Wendy the Wedding Planner cozy mystery series.

Cindy has always loved reading, but it is only recently that she has discovered her passion for writing romantic cozy mysteries. She loves walking along the beach thinking of the next adventure her characters can embark on.

You can sign up for her newsletter so you are notified of her latest releases at http://www.cindybellbooks.com.

ALSO BY CINDY BELL

CHOCOLATE CENTERED COZY MYSTERIES

The Sweet Smell of Murder

A Deadly Delicious Delivery

A Bitter Sweet Murder

A Treacherous Tasty Trail

Pastry and Peril

Trouble and Treats

Fudge Films and Felonies

Custom-Made Murder

Skydiving, Soufflés and Sabotage

Christmas Chocolates and Crimes

Hot Chocolate and Homicide

Chocolate Caramels and Conmen

Picnics, Pies and Lies

Devils Food Cake and Drama

Cinnamon and a Corpse

Cherries, Berries and a Body

Christmas Cookies and Criminals

Grapes, Ganache & Guilt

DUNE HOUSE COZY MYSTERIES

Seaside Secrets

Boats and Bad Guys

Treasured History

Hidden Hideaways

Dodgy Dealings

Suspects and Surprises

Ruffled Feathers

A Fishy Discovery

Danger in the Depths

Celebrities and Chaos

Pups, Pilots and Peril

Tides, Trails and Trouble

Racing and Robberies

Athletes and Alibis

Manuscripts and Deadly Motives

Pelicans, Pier and Poison

Sand, Sea and a Skeleton

Pianos and Prison

WAGGING TAIL COZY MYSTERIES

Murder at Pawprint Creek (prequel)

Murder at Pooch Park

Murder at the Pet Boutique

A Merry Murder at St. Bernard Cabins

Murder at the Dog Training Academy

Murder at Corgi Country Club

A Merry Murder on Ruff Road

Murder at Poodle Place

Murder at Hound Hill

Murder at Rover Meadows

SAGE GARDENS COZY MYSTERIES

Sage Gardens Cozy Mystery Series Box Set Volume 1 (Books 1 - 4)

Birthdays Can Be Deadly

Money Can Be Deadly

Trust Can Be Deadly

Ties Can Be Deadly

Rocks Can Be Deadly

Jewelry Can Be Deadly

Numbers Can Be Deadly

Memories Can Be Deadly

Paintings Can Be Deadly

Snow Can Be Deadly

Tea Can Be Deadly

Greed Can Be Deadly

Clutter Can Be Deadly

NUTS ABOUT NUTS COZY MYSTERIES

A Tough Case to Crack

A Seed of Doubt

Roasted Peanuts and Peril

Chestnuts, Camping and Culprits

DONUT TRUCK COZY MYSTERIES

Deadly Deals and Donuts

Fatal Festive Donuts

Bunny Donuts and a Body

Strawberry Donuts and Scandal

Frosted Donuts and Fatal Falls

BEKKI THE BEAUTICIAN COZY MYSTERIES

Hairspray and Homicide

A Dyed Blonde and a Dead Body

Mascara and Murder

Pageant and Poison

Conditioner and a Corpse

Mistletoe, Makeup and Murder

Hairpin, Hair Dryer and Homicide

Blush, a Bride and a Body

Shampoo and a Stiff

Cosmetics, a Cruise and a Killer

Lipstick, a Long Iron and Lifeless

Camping, Concealer and Criminals

Treated and Dyed

A Wrinkle-Free Murder

A MACARON PATISSERIE COZY MYSTERY SERIES

Sifting for Suspects

Recipes and Revenge

Mansions, Macarons and Murder

HEAVENLY HIGHLAND INN COZY MYSTERIES

Murdering the Roses

Dead in the Daisies

Killing the Carnations

Drowning the Daffodils

Suffocating the Sunflowers

Books, Bullets and Blooms

A Deadly Serious Gardening Contest

A Bridal Bouquet and a Body

Digging for Dirt

WENDY THE WEDDING PLANNER COZY MYSTERIES

Matrimony, Money and Murder

Chefs, Ceremonies and Crimes

Knives and Nuptials

Mice, Marriage and Murder

TESSA'S VANILLA CAKE RECIPE

Ingredients:

Cake

1 1/2 sticks (3/4 cup) butter softened to room temperature
1 1/2 cups superfine sugar
4 eggs at room temperature
2 tablespoons vanilla extract
3 cups all-purpose flour
1/2 teaspoon baking soda
2 teaspoons baking powder
1 1/2 cups buttermilk at room temperature

Vanilla Frosting

TESSA'S VANILLA CAKE RECIPE

2 sticks (1 cup) butter
2 tablespoons milk
4 cups confectioners' sugar sifted
4 teaspoons vanilla extract

Preparation:

Preheat the oven to 350 degrees Fahrenheit.

Butter and line the base of 2 x 9 inch round cake pans.

Beat the butter and superfine sugar together until smooth and creamy.

Add the eggs one at a time and mix until well-combined.

Add the vanilla extract.

In another bowl sift together the all-purpose flour, baking powder and baking soda.

Gradually add the dry ingredients, alternating with the buttermilk, to the butter mixture.

TESSA'S VANILLA CAKE RECIPE

Divide the mixture between the prepared cake pans.

Bake in the pre-heated oven for 20 - 25 minutes, until a skewer inserted into the middle comes out clean.

Leave the cakes to cool in the cake pans for about 10 minutes and then remove from the pans and cool on a wire rack. Once cooled remove parchment paper from the base of the cakes.

To make the vanilla frosting, in a large bowl beat the butter until creamy. Gradually add the sifted confectioners' sugar and mix until well combined. Mix in the milk and the vanilla extract.

Top one of the cakes with the vanilla frosting and place the other on top. Spread the frosting over the top and sides of the cake.

Enjoy!!

Printed in Great Britain
by Amazon